A Tale of an Arctic Atlantis

A tale to be told round the fire hearths as the snow-daemons howl and prowl about, of were-whales and tree-tigers, of the bewitchments of the Painted Men (whose skin must not be seen), of those fell compacts which bind their members to go a-roving and a-robbing. . . .

A story that perhaps should be told in tones low and grave, such that listeners must need pile high the fires again and sometimes yet again—for warmth, for courage, comfort, drawing nearer to each other and nearer yet: till each could see in every other eye the reflection of the dancing flames. . . .

This tale of Ursus of Ultima Thule.

Avram Davidson

URSUS
of Ultima Thule

AVON
PUBLISHERS OF BARD, CAMELOT, DISCUS, EQUINOX AND FLARE BOOKS

URSUS OF ULTIMA THULE is an original publication of Avon Books. This work has never before appeared in book form.

AVON BOOKS
A division of
The Hearst Corporation
959 Eighth Avenue
New York, New York 10019

First Avon Printing, December, 1973.

Printed in the U.S.A.

URSUS
of Ultima Thule

If even continents drift and flow, it is not surprising that names of places should do the same. There is, for example: Britain, North Britain (Scotland), West Britain (Ireland), Great Britain (England, Wales and Scotland), Brittany (in France), and New Britain (a city in Connecticut and a large island near New Guinea). There was also Thule. Where was Thule? Was it the Orkney Islands? Norway? Iceland? Suppose there was not only the Thule of Pytheas, but long, long before Pytheas . . . a Farther Thule . . . a Farthest Thule . . . in short, another Thule entirely. Old Thule. The original Thule. And suppose that theory to be correct, which holds that within the lifetime of homo sapien the poles and polar zones underwent a great shift. And so suppose that buried under the all but immemorial ice of the interior of one of the great Arctic islands (say Spitzbergen . . . Nova Zemlya . . . Greenland . . .) lies buried, forever beyond our reach and ken, the remnants of an ancient race and culture: that of the people of Thule. Old Thule. Ultimate Thule. An Arctic Atlantis, immersed beneath ice instead of ocean.

This, then, is a tale of the original Ultima Thule—before its people fled the most invincible of enemies; before—long before—they fled south, and farther south again: there, either to be obliterated by (or, likelier, absorbed by) other men

7

and other cultures—their very tongue and speech forgotten. One word alone survives, thrown up like a piece of rack or wreckage upon an inhospitable shore: a word now part of every language, though now traceable to none: the name of their lost and ancient homeland: Thule.

PREAMBLE

Long, long before the sun had moved her circle and her path and cliffs of ice descended forever upon true and Farthest Thule, Arntenas Arnten (he who could speak the language of the Bear and of the great red mammonts) ruled there: and he held the ultimate rule in that land-whole of the nains and the perries, and was King of the Men, and of the Other Men as well. Neither Picts nor Celts nor Scands nor Wends nor Finnds had come as yet to the Southern Lands below, nor had any of those lands sunk as yet beneath the all-circling sea.

Elk drew his sledges swiftly over the mossy turf in summer and upon the silver snows of winter, and he was wealthy in gold and amber and his nains had the art of crafting for him blades which never suffered from either the green sickness or the red. This was done inland, sometimes in the forest and sometimes on the heath. And the shores of the all-circling sea saw, in guarded coves, the perries working most skillfully in colored glass, but seldom if ever could men see them, for they slipped like shadows into the rocks and clefts, and they blended like shadows into the trees, for such is the manner and the form of the perries. And in the king's hall the people feast upon the flesh of salmons and of stags, whilst the great dire wolves—who eat from the king's own hand alone—prowl in both the outer and the inner court to the king's own chambers.

Past the forest and the heath are the Paar Marches, and past the Paar Marches are the Death Marshes and the Great Glens where the wizards dwell: and none but they (save, of course, the king) have the way to the Deep Caves, the airs of which both are intermittently foul and often fatal. It is when lightning strikes those rotting airs and thick murk mists that dragons are gendered. And as to what use these dragons are put, these are not the proper concerns of either nains or perries or Men or Other Man, and certainly not of the bar-bar-folk who come at times a-prowling o'er the all-circling sea; but only of the wizards and the king. Often do his singing-women beg him to relate them somewhat of the wonders said to bide there. If he is of a good mood he passes it off with a bauble or a jest, and if he is of an ill mood he may fling a sandal or a buskin at them with a rough word. Sometimes, if his mood is grom, he tells them such tales as makes them shriek and hold their ears and beg for leave to go. But if his mood is very grom indeed he makes them to tarry and to listen and to bide.

Other tales are told round the fire hearths as the snow-daemons howl and prowl about, of were-whales and tree-tigers, of the bewitchments of the Painted Men (whose skin must not be seen), of those fell compacts which bind their members to go a-roving and a-robbing and at last to pile all their troves and treasures in one great heap and fight by two and day by day till only one survives: winner take all; the king's men and the king's guests sing in Deep Chant of the cult of the Divine and Dying Bear, who descends into death each winter and who rises from his grave again at each winter-end ... at length their chant itself dies down and they gaze all silent into the embers and sometimes without mickle more than a murmur they roll them in their furs and fleeces and sigh their way to sleep ...

But sometimes someone in tones low and grave would half-tell, half-whisper such a story that the listeners must need pile high the fires again and sometimes yet again—for warmth, for courage, comfort, or perhaps to mark the passing time—drawing nonetheless nearer to each other and nearer, nearer yet: till each could see in every other eye the reflection of the dancing flames ... the darting flames ... the dancing, darting, wondering flames.

Chapter I

In the darkness of his granduncle's medicine hut by the flickerflicker of the faint fire (which the man was allowed to have, grudgingly, and at high tax, for preparing his simple witcheries) the boy recollected the sound of the taptap beats on the tiny witchery-drum and the sight of the mandrakes lifting the lid of their bark box house and coming out to dance by the fire, tossing up their small-small scrannel arms and stamping their tiny-tiny feet to the toom-*toom*, toom-*toom*, toom-*toom*-petty-*toom* of the child-sized drum—then dancing backward and closing the lid on themselves as the last faint pulse beat died away.

A small man, his uncle or granduncle (in those days the boy did not distinguish), with a skill in small witcheries and small magics by which he sustained them. And the boy felt proud of seeing what other boys did not see.

But most of his memories before the breakaway were ill ones.

When he grew big enough to wander from the partly underground medicine hut or the round thatched house where his uncle's sister sat mumbling as she pounded bark or stirred the acorn gruel, the boy learned swiftly enough how little he had to pride himself in. If you are smaller by far than the smallest of any born in your birth year, if they are smooth of skin and fair of hair and you are dark and your swarthy skin is covered with a nap or bloom of dark hair—are these things to be proud of? If others have fathers and brothers who return from the hunt to be greeted by the singing of their women and if your only family connection with it all is when old uncle or old uncle's sister comes stooping up and waits for a bone or an offal to be tossed as to a dog—is there pride in this?

To be sure, he was quicker of body and sharper of mind than any of his birth year; sharp and quick enough to learn that sharpness and quickness won praise only for others and in him were only to be resented. That magic and witchery produced fear and that fear often produced respect; but that small-scale magic and witchery caused only small fear—suspicion, rather—and hardly ever respect at all. For fear and fears hung over the town like the smoke from the great central fire on lowering days. Fear that someone was working a witchery, fear of the wild ones of the woods, fear of the king and the tax-gatherers, fear of known magic and of unknown even more. And the boy who was small and sharp and dark and shaggy produced an effect of strangeness like the subtle smell of fear—but was not strong enough to ward off the hates and wraths this caused—and besides—and besides . . .

The affair of the great roan mammont, the rogue mammont, fear of fears and terror of terrors, brought all things to a head. But before that, long-long before that day of blood and death, that day of the hill-that-moved, the trees-that-walk, serpent-snout and spear-teeth and all the other names used when one dares not use the real name: *mam-*

14

mont; long before then, when he was very small, there was the token.

The token hung on a thong from a peg in a post in his grandmother's hut. For a while it was above his head and he reached for it often while the old one squatted, mumbling, in the sun of the doorfront. He could not remember the first time he actually reached it, standing on a stool (probably), but he had a clear recollection of one day scanning it and seeing it and recognizing it. It was carved of wood, roughly but forcefully, in the form of a bear. It had the bear's head and one tooth showed clearly in the crude snout; it had the bear's paws and legs.

But the legs ended in the feet of a man.

Perhaps at that time he had not recognized this strangeness; he had certainly never seen a bear, for it was not till later that Tall Roke brought in the cub that was partly petted and partly tortured until it was abruptly killed and eaten. Likely at that child-time he did not know that a bear has bear's feet and that although they resemble a man's, yet they are not. Nor was it yet clear to him how subtly manlike the carving was.

But he had the clear recollection of scanning it that one day and becoming aware that the old woman, granduncle's sister and his own grandmother, had come in and was staring at him, a look on her blear and withered face odd even for her on whom odd looks were common. A look of fear and love and awe and horror.

Sensing that she was in what was for her a lucid mood, he asked as he pointed, "This—what?"

And she, promptly and matter-of-factly, said, "Your father." And as promptly thrust awry her snaggle-snarl hair and screamed and rolled her rheumy eyes and tore open the bosom of her bark-cloth dress and beat and scratched her withered dugs and wailed and howled and beat her head upon the earthen floor. "Hinna!" she screamed. "Hinna! Hinna!" and, "Hinna-tenna!"

Such fits and antics were not so rare as to alarm the boy—for all he knew, all grandmothers behaved so—just as, for all he knew, all fathers were carved of wood and hung on leather thongs from posts. But this fit was uncommonly severe and he appreciated, in fact he rather enjoyed, the new aspects of it, as he might have enjoyed a new grip noted in a dog fight.

Hinna. So the old man sometimes addressed the old woman. Sometimes the old woman said it as she pointed out the small blue flowers of a plant occasionally brought back with other herbs and roots or leaves and barks from the woods by the old man. So: Hinna was the old woman and hinna was a flower, but he knew that this old woman was not thrown into a fit in order to mention either; he did not know *how* he knew and wondered, mildly, that he knew at all. Logic was here working scarcely above the level of intuition.

The old woman shrieked and babbled "Woe!" but mostly her words were strange and, "*Hinna-tenna!*" she screamed. And, "*Arn't! Arn't Arn't!*"

And then old Bab-uncle was kneeling beside her, soothing her, calming her, arranging her tattered dress of pounded bark-lining, carrying her at last—when her voice was a mere croon or drone—to the

16

worn-almost-hairless half of deerhide which covered her grass bed. And the old man got up and seemed at a loss as he looked at the boy who sensed and instantly seized an opportunity.

Pointing to the token on the thong, "My father," he said.

"Yes," said the old man, unsurprised. Then he winced.

What made the boy say what he next said, still pointing? No knowing—unless it was unrealized awareness of a connection between strange things enclosed in a space of time—such as this moment which had just passed, or perhaps still was passing.

Pointing to the token he said, "Arn't. Arn't."

"Arn," his uncle said, absentminded correction in his tone.

So. *Arn* was the token that was the bear that was his father and his father had somehow thrown the old woman into a fit in which *Arn't* was somehow different. And what else was in the fit which was familiar yet different—for something was.

Ah.

"*Tenna,*" the boy said, immediately correcting himself: "*Hinna-tenna.*"

Without so much as a sigh and in the same flat, abstracted voice in which he would explain to a visitor at the medicine hut the care and feeding of mandrakes or the price of a charm or the manner of a charm (other men whose work was witchery had the better sense to sink their voices and roll their eyes and make at least a few fearful gestures and whisper at least a few words dolefully, lips to ear. Other witcherers commanded higher prices, too, got amber-grains and goodly pelts, were not content with bones and offals) his granduncle said to him, "Hinna is the cornflower and is also my sister's name. Your grandmother. Was her daughter's name. Your mother. *Tenna* is a word in the Old Tongue, now archaic, used chiefly for witchery. Spoken sometimes by such relics as myself and sister. Tenna means 'daughter.' *Arn* in the older tongue is 'bear.' So, now I consider it, *Arn't'* may be applied to the token, for my sister's daughter said she had it of the bear. As she said, too, she had you. But she was never right in her wits after that and grew worse and we found her drowned."

After a moment he nodded once or twice and left the house without more word, confident, apparently, that he had said everything there was to be said. As, perhaps, he had.

The boy realized, growing older, that often he himself saw sequences and connections where other boys saw none. But just as he could see logic and they not, just so things that seemed sensible to them were senseless and unpredictable to him. More than once he had been stoned away from following hunters, yet today he had been asked—not allowed, *asked*—"Come, honey-dripper, bring us good luck!" And here he was with the rest of them in the high grass and the sun hot upon the earth and on them all so that he could smell it and them and the grass and other things not even seen.

Honey-dripper, with a guffaw. It was a name for him. *Comb-robber* was another. Both meant *bear*, who stole the honeycomb from the honey tree and ate it, dripping its richness, grubs and wax and all. But *comb-robber*, applied to him, was merely an

18

ill-name. *Honey-dripper* was less so, was a laughing term, and—somehow—referred not exclusively to the bear but also had something to do with men and the things men had with women. Tall Roke it was who'd said him this name this day and asked him to come; and Tall Roke it was, when another had looked black and muttered, who had briskly and blithely answered, "What? For that some rough fellow tumbled his mad mother and gamed her, saying, 'I'm a bear!' What? A bigger fool than she or you I'd be to think the kid an ill-bringer for that. Ah no, but that his old uncle's witchery had maybe rubbed off on him a bit, and then a-smells as wild as any beasty and so may cover our own man-stinks—"

But as yet the boy could not smell the wild white horses they were hunting—the swift, mane-tossing, clever-cunning, clever-mad, mad-eyed, red-eyed, wild-eyed, wild, white horses—whom no man's mind or hand had ever yet thought to tame. Three days since, some village stripling, gaming about in the meadows, had found a colt with its leg broken in a mole hole, had swiftly (but, be sure, not without a swifter, fearful lookabout) cut its throat and borne it home. Perhaps one of its marrowbones was still stewing in a pot of spelt; the rest had sure been eaten. But the clever-mad horses of the herd had tracked the lostling down to its place of injury, had seen the blood, had traced the drips of blood as far to the village as even their mad courage cared to go. Since then they had been waging war; trampling crops, attacking cultivators and wanderers with hooves and teeth. So now the menfolk were carrying the war unto the horsefolk.

19

Time was when only the poorest of the poor would have had stone or bone for his weapons. All else had had iron—had even had arrow or spear-heads to spare, in case of breakage before a wandernain (some called them "shamblenain," but not to their faces) would come trading new irons for old; amber and peltries their fee: taking the broken points with them back to strange and distant Nainland to mend upon their witchery-forge, an art that only the nains had. As for bronze, that was only a memory, bronze had long since died of the green-sickness. As yet, out here, the deadly rust was moving slowly, but move it did; something was deadly wrong with iron, and no nains came; grim was the mood of the distant king, and—

"Hist, now," said Tall Roke. "Mind the plan, now. Drive away the young stallions and the mares with stones, the colts will follow—cut off the great stallion, and whilst we three engage him from in front, you two cut his tendons from behind." The great stallion, with hamstrings severed on his hind legs, would go down and never rise. Deprived of leader, the other steeds would flee.

Tall Roke hawked and spat and grunted. He needed not to point. They had come to the edge of the escarpment and in the near distance of the wide, shallow valley, they saw the horses like wee white clouds floating in the blue-green sky of grass. For a moment they gazed, the five or six full men, the twice-that-many striplings and the boy who had no name. Then they spread out widely and began the slow and cautious descent from the rim. Slow, for there was no swift going down that uncertain slope; cautious, because they dared not give alarm to the horse herd.

The boy felt for the pouch with the stones in it. The touch was reassuring. Nothing else was. His first hunt. His heart pounding. It had been agreed that any needed signaling would take the form of a ground squirrel's whistling, as this would (at most) arouse the hunger of no creature larger than a fox or hawk. Tentatively the boy formed his mouth to make such a signal. But he never made it. The while he had been keeping a sort of sketch of things in his head. Yonder was the sun. The cliff directly behind. The wind, so. To the right must be the horse herd. A little left of straight ahead were, though now not seen, a clump of thick-boled trees. Beyond that, a low hillock of rusty scrub. A brook. A wallow.

Alarm, alarm rose so swift in his chest that it choked his breath. Something was wrong. Everything was wrong. He had gone the wrong way—or—for he was much too close to the hillock, he could see it now, he could not see the trees, which meant—and then came the whistle, and the whistle was to have come from Tall Roke and Tall Roke should be *that* way and the whistle was over *this* way—vertigo took him, he was on both knees and one hand. Earthshake? For the hillock moved and his eyes fled from it and his eyes saw trees walking and someone screamed and screamed—it was not him, then it *was* him as it was many others, for by now all knew it was *the hill-that-moves, the trees-that-walk,* all of them could see the *serpent snout* that rose up huge and hairy and drank the wind, all

21

could see the flash of *spear teeth*, all could hear the horrid trumpet scream of the *mammont! mammont! mammont!* as its tree-huge legs shook the grassy ground in its terrible charge, its trunk sweeping down the grass before it as a scythe, bloody scythe, bloody grass, bloody spears, bloody teeth—

Fear and failing flesh and yet senses still undimmed enough to hear Tall Roke's voice full strong as he shouted, "Hold to the plan! Axe men to the rear whilst I engage to the front—" *I* and not *we*, he did not trust to any others' courage to face the huge red mammont from the front, but still had hopes that some might brave the great beast's hind legs to strike at the lower tendons. Onward the mammont beast had come, fast, fast, but faster yet ran Tall Roke, passing it—so swift he might have escaped, had such been his intent, had he run in another direction—passing it, running backward before it, turning it, darting back and away from it, shouting and feinting his spear at it—"Strike! Strike!" he shouted—

But no one was there to strike. No one was there but Tall Roke. One man. One boy. Who shrieked with all the fury of his unformed voice and cast his stones with all the power of his unformed arms. For one fell moment the mammont wavered, rage-reddened eyes darting from man to boy.

"Ankles! Ankles! Ah! Strike! Ankles!" hoarsely but still hopefully: Tall Roke's voice. But no one struck. And the one man's spear hung in the air, it seemed not so much that he had cast it at the mammont as that the mammont had hurled itself upon the airborne spear; it lanced the line of the great face from tusk-socket to eye-socket: the mammont screamed its pain and rage: again the spear hung in the air: and now—and this was so puzzling—Tall Roke himself hung in the air, his fair hair all in a mist about his face—the python trunk seemed to rise slowly, slowly, slowly, and to descend slowly, slowly, and to wrap itself so slowly gently lovingly about the man's neck.

There were flowers in the meadow and bees in the air and then there was a dripping comb of honey and he thrust his paws first into the comb and then into his mouth and its taste was of gold and sweet and strong and delightful beyond the taste of any food tasted before and when it was quite quite gone he licked his paws and he licked the grass it had dripped on and then he went scampering off to where the bushes hung heavy with the full ripe berries and he ate his wonder full of them and . . .

Three of them returned alive to the village and Tall Roke was found alive (though only barely) where the mammont had tossed and gored him but, unaccountably, not trampled him as it had the others. But he, too, was soon dead. Another's head was found in the branches of a tree. Something that was probably his body, for it could be nothing else, was smeared nearby.

The horses had vanished.

That the great roan mammont was a rogue, all agreed. Only a rogue would travel alone, and there was no sign at all of any other mammont—or, for that matter, him—any more.

At first no one in the village said anything but, *It has happened.* Since the starting of the red-rust-sickness of all iron and the increasing wrath of the distant and once indifferent king, since the nains had ceased to visit and the tax exactions had begun to increase, rumors faint as whispers and whispers loud as shouts had been spreading, spreading, spreading. Some great calamity impended. And now it had come. It had happened.

Next in the village they began to ask, *How did it happen?*

By this time the boy thought he knew. And there was one other who, he thought, also thought he knew. And that meant there was a third who certainly knew.

The name of the second was Corm, a lad perhaps a year or two older, eyes gray rather than the common blue, hair not blond and curling but brown and lank, sallow of skin; his father was one of the three subchiefs of the townlet. If Corm had not given the boy many good words, that was nothing, no one did that; but he had never given any ill ones at all.

The third was a whey-faced, slack-mouthed, slack-limbed shambleton, with an almost perpetual eruption about the mouth at which he ever picked and which generally bled; a liar and bully and boor, yet well connected—that is, connected to families of some small importance who, by talking loud and often and big, made that small seem greater.

It was one of those moments that seem to have been a part of the center of all things, lying in wait from the beginning. No hint of it before. Old

Hinna's grandson standing idly watching. Whey-face shambling along. The boy looking at him. Looking up to see Corm watching Whey-face as well. His eyes meeting Corm's. Instantly, as though spoken words had passed between them: *It was Whey-face who gave that first, wrong whistle, which would have been done right if Tall Roke had done it at the right time if it should have been done at all; it came from where Whey-face was, and only he would have been fool enough, coward enough to have done it, done it in coward-fool hopes of a reassuring return of it: it was that whistle, ill-done, that roused the mammont—in another moment Tall Roke would have seen it and managed to get us all safe away somehow, but—*

Still that same second, Whey-face looking up as though called, catching their glance, understanding, flushing, paling, and at once reacting in his coward way—not coward-foolish this time but coward-cunning. Pointing at the boy, shouting at the boy, attracting instantly every eye and mind voicing the unvoiced and making clamor become instant fact: "It was *him! He* brought the ill-fate, *he* brought the mammont there! The bear's bastard with the bear-stink on him! Bear's bastard! Nain's get! Made the mammont come! Curse-bringer! Shag-skin! Killed our men and boys! *Him! Him! Him!*" And, stooping, he snatched up a piece of dried filth, ran and flung it.

Then sticks, then stones. Next would-be arrows, axes, spears. No need to inquire, discuss, reason, weigh—instant, heart-warming hatred was quick, easy. *"Bear's bastard! Curse-bringer! Men killed! Bear-stink!"* The mammont was gone, the boy re-

25

mained. He saw Corm's mouth open but neither he nor any heard Corm's word, drowned out in the bull-voiced clamor of all of Whey-face's kith and kin, believing or not believing, belief beside the point, the point: Ours. Support him. Shout loud. Throw something.

The boy ran. Terror runs swifter than rage follows. Boys can go where big men cannot—holes, hollows, runways, dogpaths, shinny up slender trees and drop over palings. There was Bab-uncle crouching up his slender fire. It was an instant. His grandmother's hut. A packet thrust into his hands, the bark bag with the small victuals the old man took with him when he hunted herbs. A hide lifted up to show an opening the boy had never seen before. A burrow, wide enough for him. A patch of light. The village palisades behind him. An echoing that might have been the clamor of the mob. That might have been the beating of his blood. Something clutched in his other hand. He ran. He ran.

Chapter II

"Go, Arnten. Find your father," the old uncle had said as he lifted the hide-flap. As it fell and all was dark, the boy heard him say, "It is time." Then nothing but a faint moment of one of the old man's chantings. *Arnten.* The word lodged like a grub in a honeycomb cell. *Arnten.* But there was no sign, yet. A faint thought: *it is my name.* No time

26

for further thought. *Arnten*. His name. That and escape. For now, enough. A life. A name.

In the woods, however, nothing was now asking his name. With a knowledge deeper than thought he avoided the hard-trodden dust of the common path and sank into the thicket like a snake. Behind, he heard the clamor and shouting descend into a single sound on a single note and stay there, like the noise of a swarm of bees hovering and *mrumming* its one dull note forever. Somehow it sounded infinitely more menacing than any cluster of mere words. Presently the humming-*mrumming* grew louder. Then loud. The ear-pressed earth echoed like a drumhead. The echo filled the ear and air. Suddenly it was gone and he, Arnten, realized that it had gone a time ago and that he was alone and that if any were still seeking him, they were not doing it here.

Slowly he rose up in the thicket like a mist. He gained the path. He snuffed up the breeze. He listened. He was gone.

A bird sang twit-twit-*twit* on a branch. A ground squirrel hopped and scampered, scampered and hopped, vanished from view. There was a smell of wetness, of damp earth and the scent of the sweet green breath of plants. Arnten knew that there were times to look up and times to look down and times to look straight ahead. He saw the bush, he saw through the bush and, a long, long way beyond the bush, he saw the boles of several trees but nothing in between. Softly, gently, he pushed the shrubby branches aside. For a moment he paused, holding his breath, listening. There was not, had

27

not been for long, sounds of mob or pack or crowd. There had been no man sounds at all, save for his own. It was improbable that any enemy of his own blood was near. It was not impossible.

But he heard no new noise. Only the faint patter of the ground squirrel. Only the same twit-twit-*twit* of the bird on the branch.

He slipped past the handful of branches and let them make their own return to their natural positions, only restraining them enough so that they should close without sound. He went on a bit and then he stopped and considered, there in the cool green corridor which for now meant safety. It had been used enough to create a trail, but little enough to allow the bush's growing to obscure the entrance. Perhaps small and dainty deer slipped along this tunnel through the trees. They would not mind sharing it with him. Or perhaps white tiger, dire wolf, snowy leopard, used it in quest of the same small dainty deer. This thought contracted and shook his limbs in a long shudder. He felt and saw the nap of hair quiver upon his skin and stand up from the fearful flesh.

His mind leaped from thought to thought as a spark of fire leaps from one twig to another. Another boy, conceiving the same thought, might find his mind working *thought of danger—beast equals danger—beast equals panic—run for your life*, without even realizing the process. But his own mind worked *thought of danger—beast equals* think *about danger—beast*. And he stopped and thought.

The thought is not the thing.

And the thought told him that the thing, the great ones among the danger-beasts, were seldom if ever to be found in this part of Thule at this season of the year; they were to be found (or rather, avoided) farther to the north, where men had less thinned out the game on which they chiefly preyed; winter snows, in which the hooved beasts would flounder and be more easily tracked and trapped and killed, might indeed bring the great killers down.

But then again might not.

He felt the drum within his bosom slow its clamor and then its beats receded to their normal slow strokes, below the threshhold of perception. He began to go on, but the trail was narrow and something caught upon a branch and held him. He looked down and saw he was still carrying without awareness the two things hastily taken in his flight from town. The bark bag of food, the bear-token upon its leathern thong. It was this last he now had to disengage. It seemed somehow as natural to hang it around his neck as to loop the grass cord of the food wallet from shoulder to hip. So. He had no weapon but he had food, itself a sort of weapon—was not hunger the chief enemy? He had a potency in the form of the bear carving, a token of whoever his father was—a father contained in a piece of wood on a thong was better than no father at all. *Find your father, Arnten.* What did he know of how or where? Either his father was or was not a bear. If not, then he knew and could know nothing. If so—then what? Where were bears? Anywhere, manywhere, where there were trees and streams. So. Avoid the grasslands, the great meadows. But he would have done so in any case. There was the game he could not take, there would be the great beasts, the danger-beasts he could not forfend.

Therefore, the forest. A tree creaked. It seemed a Yes.

When the balls of boiled millet and scraps of dried meat and fish were gone from his bark bag he went a while without and he hungered. Then there were berries and plants his old herb-uncle had shown him. He ate walking and he slept little. He seemed to need less of either. If the path forked and one branch inclined toward the plains of danger, he took the other. If there was still a choice and a question, he held the token in his hands and pointed it between the paths. It moved. Sometimes slowly, slightly. But it moved. It had one day not yet stopped moving when he felt the eyes upon him and looked up. They were great, glowing, amber eyes—intelligent eyes, but far too strange to be the eyes of any man. Nor were they.

The figure was squat of body and shag of skin, with a brown mane of hair upon scalp and broad face. The extraordinarily long arms were folded across the extraordinarily thick chest. A kilt of soft leather girdled the loins. Short were the powerful legs. Over arms, hands and chest and belly the long brown hair grew thickly. The boy found himself looking at his own body and limbs. Instantly, several thoughts—and one of them as an almost instant surprise: *I am not afraid!* And, another—

"Nay, boy." The voice was strange in more than being unknown. It had odd tones and echoes, the final vowels nasalized so that almost they sounded as *nay'n, boy'n.* "Nay, boy. It's isn't me nurr any we

30

who's is fathered ye 'n given 'e them warm hairs upon yurr's skin." So acutely did the strange one discern his thoughts. And spoke a few words of no understanding, at first, to the boy—whose ear sped back and caught on a word he knew.

"*Arn't.*"

He said, "The bear—"

Something flashed golden in the amber eyes. More strange words. Then— "Ye dow int speak en witchery words—hey'n?" Arnten shook his head. "Nay," murmured the stranger. Almost, it was *Ngayng.* He said, "We speak it ever 't'the forge. Ye must's ever speak en 't' th' Old Tongue t'iron, furr iron 't's a witchery thing. So we speak en it furr habit, ef we dow int think not to—"

"You said—'*Arn't*'—"

"Eh. We speak 's'en it, too, 't the bear, furr the bear dow be a witchery-beast. All creaturr dow die, but the bear dow come alive agains. And the Star Bear dow gived we-folk the first fire." The glowing eyes fixed his own. The odd voice, strong and strange, but devoid of harm for him, went on. "En all of Thule's the wurrd gone round, '*When the wolf dow meet the bear: beware.*' " There seemed something expectant in his tone, something expectant in his look.

But look and tone alike meant nothing to the boy, who said, as though thinking aloud, "A nain." The nain stooped his head and his shoulders. And the boy said, "Arnten, I am Arnten." And this time the nain stooped his entire thick body to the waist.

Then, straightening, he extended an arm so long that its fingers almost touched Arnten's chest. "We know en what place 't is." The boy's eyes followed and saw the thick and hairy fingers of the thick and hairy hand were pointing not to his body but to the token slung upon it.

"Where? It is *here*."

The nain grunted, held up a hand straight from the wrist in the nain sign of negation. "Not this. Th' other this. Th'—th'—" He struggled to express himself, his manner rather like that of a man seeking a paraphrase for a thing he does not care to name precisely. "Th' *other* this. *That!*"

And he turned and walked away.

Arnten followed.

After a full seven-days' walk they came to it. The place was more of a hole or cleft than a cave, but it was dry. Part of the ceiling had fallen in; boulders littered the floor. The nain without hesitating or pausing put his chest against the largest and wound long arms around it. He moved the stone up and over and then back. "Take 't up," he said. " 'T's not furr we to touch." *It*, clearly, was not the rock. A moment passed in the dim light before Arnten saw *it*. For a moment he thought it was a piece of wood. Then, more by intuition than lineal recognition, he knew that what he saw on the ground where the rock had been was a witchery-bundle.

That.

It was perhaps the size of his forearm and, with his forearm, after he had taken it outside in the sunlight, he wiped at the dusty hide covering. It was certainly a witchery-bundle. There were witchery signs upon it, some clear, some dim, some familiar, some unknown. Largest and most deeply

32

etched were the sun and the bear. The bear was almost certainly a replica of the one he wore. Or—was
it the other way around? "The sun," he said.

"Eh'ng," the nain agreed. "The sun and the bear,
they go together. For the sun dies and 't comes
alive again. And the bear dow die and dow come
alive again. The sun give fire and the bear, too.
Eh'ng," he said, after a moment, eyeing the hide-
covered bundle, and musing. "How many snow-
times? Two hands? Surely two. But three? Surely
not three. Bear, he telled a-we, Here dow be my token. Here dow by my," the nain gestured, "*that*.
Bear telled: 'Look for it. If you see him, man-
child-bearchild—if you see my token on 't him;
show him where.' And we say'd him, Eh'ng-ah,
Bear."

It was mystery, but it was good mystery. Witchery, but he could not think it any but good witchery. It was a good moment. Why, then, did the
flood of bad memory rise up in his mind, come spill-
ing out of his mouth? "They stoned me. They pelt-
ed me with filth. They called me *nain's get* and
bear's bastard and they tried to kill me."

The nain's amber-colored eyes glowed and dark-
ened and in level sunlight glowed like a beast's in
the night, glowed red, glowed like an amber in the
nighttime fire.

Words like distant thunder rolled in his vast
chest and rumbled in his wide throat.

"Wolf's lice! Accursed smoothskins!" He spoke
at last in the common tongue and continued to do
so, though occasionally dropping into naintalk or
the archaic language of witchery. "If it were not
for us and our iron they would still be eating of
33

grubs and lizards and roots. And what will they do now, as iron dies? Is there one of them, a single one even, with cunning and courage enough to feed the wizards? Their king, ah, he might have, when he was young, but he's gotten old now, he's gotten half-mad now, he looks in the wrong direction, he afflicts where no affliction can help, the wind blows cruel hard from the north but he thinks it blows from the south! A nain's life is that it's worth to try to persuade him—if a nain wished it. As for the rest of the slim race—" He caught his breath, part in a sigh, part in a sob. The fiery glow in his eyes began to die away.

"Nay, I'll say no more as regards that race and blood, 'tis partly yours. They may deny it, may deny you—you may wish to deny it and them. But the blood cannot be denied. Nay, nay. The blood cannot be denied." Abruptly, gesturing to the bundle, the nain said, "Open it then."

The outer covering had been tied tight with sinews, but his probing fingers found one loose enough to allow his teeth purchase. He gnawed, felt the fibers give way—give until his teeth met with a click. Quickly his fingernails pulled the thread, tugged it from pierced hole, from the next and next. Some sort of dried membrane—the bladder, perhaps, of a large animal—was inside the outer covering, bound about with bark cord which did not long resist attack. Inside was a long pouch with a drawstring tied in tassels. Carefully he unfastened this, carefully he laid out the contents on the outer wrappings.

First, by size alone, was a knife in a sheath of horn and leather, with a good bone handle carved in the same likeness of a bear. It was entirely unaffected by the iron-rot. It was a good knife.

There was also a dried and withered beechnut.

There was also a greenstone.

There was also a bear's claw.

There was also, bent and doubled, but not yet broken, a river reed.

There was nothing else.

He looked up to ask about these, but the nain was gone.

Every man had a witchery-bundle; even children devised them in imitation of their elders. Some had richly adorned ones, the contents bought of high-priced witcherers for nuggets of amber and pelts of marten, sable, ermine, white tigers, snow leopards. Some had but meager pouches containing perhaps a single item—a bone, a dried this-or-that, a something seen in a dream and sought for and found. A tooth pried from a dry skull. A fragment of something said to be a thunderstone.

Some had inherited.

So had he.

The knife alone would at any time have been deemed a good inheritance, the more so now that good iron was hard to find and harder to keep. The more so for the circumstances of its hiding and finding. But what did the other mean? A bear claw, now that was easy to understand. But the reed? The greenstone? *Arnten, find your father.* Had he found him? Not yet. But now, having found this much, might he not find a source? For as long—no, longer—than he himself had lived, the nains had not seen his father. He might be dead. He might be far away. He might be neither. He might be alive and very near.

Arnten carefully restored the magic items to their pouch—except for the knife, which he slung about his waist—and started off. Excitement and happiness had made him heedless and when he heard the low-voiced song in the clearing he had no thought but to see who was singing it.

It was one of the Painted Men, that was at once obvious—one of the Painted Men whom it was death to see unpainted. By greatest good fortune, though, he had just finished painting himself—and what a curious pattern his skin did present! Almost hideous. Not till the man, still humming his witchery-song, lifted his brush and dipped it in a tiny pot did Arnten realize, cold with horror, that what he was seeing was the man's naked skin!—that he had only then begun.

The Painted (or unPainted) Man swung about, panting with shame and rage. Arnten felt the club's first blow.

Chapter III

The old nain stood stolidly where the uneasy soldiers had bade him stand. He could without great effort have broken the ribs of all of them and the necks of most before any of them could stop him—and perhaps it was this that made them uneasy. But perhaps not. The king's camp and court was an uneasy place in general these days—not that the rest of Thule lay at much ease either. Slots of sunlight came through the smoke hole in the top of the great tent. The king sat back on a pelt-piled bench and the nain thought it seemed they lied who said the king was age-wasted. Indeed, as the Orfas sat there, glaring, hands clenched upon his knees, he seemed all too vigorous.

Within himself the old nain sighed a slight sigh. Only to the extent that the smoothskins were unpredictable were they predictable at all. Ah, eh. Seasons come and seasons go and ever the race of nains would remain upon the earth. Meanwhile, one endured. Heat, cold, toil, hunger, thirst, a savage beast, an unwise king.

A witchery queen.

The soldiers, fumbling and breathing their unhappiness, finished shackling the old nain's horsehide fetters to one of the roof posts, were angrily waved outside, almost stumbled over each other in their eagerness to obey.

For a long moment the king continued to glare. Then he said, slowly and with effort, but quite correctly, "Uur-tenokh-tenokh-guur."

So, this was something. At least the king remembered the nain's proper name. Or had learned it. A small courtesy, perhaps. But a courtesy. He would return it. "Orfas," he said.

The king's head snapped up with a jerk. He was not angered, he was not pleased, his attention had been called to something forgotten. Probably it had been long since he had been called by his own name in the Old Tongue, called anything (perhaps) save King or Great Bull Mammont or some other lickleg flattery such as the smoothskins used. The old nain almost without thinking essayed more syllables in the witchery language, but the king's swift gesture cut him off.

"My store of that speech has rusted in my mind," Orfas said, "as has my store of the iron you have cursed." His head shifted, his eyes flashed. "*Why* have you cursed it?"

"We have not. Do you curse your kingdom?"

"You are the High Smith of the nains. I have not had you brought here to bandy questions with me."

"You had not brought me here at all, had I not thought you would keep your word."

Bluff and bluster. What? Not kept his word? How?

"You said I would not be bound."

A false and further look of outraged pride, falling into one of faint regret and helplessness at having been stupidly misunderstood. "I said that you would not be bound with iron."

"It is by such cunning shift of words that you hope to command either my respect or my assistance?" The king flushed, either in affront or from some vestigial sense of shame. "Do you think me an owl or a bat, unable to see in daylight? I see that none of your captives are bound in iron. It is not out of any honor that I have been bound in thongs of skin, but because you no longer trust iron." It was a statement, not a question, it went home. The king looked aside, for a moment at a loss. "I will give you an advice——" The king sat up. "Sea-cow's skin is tougher by far and far less risky to hunt."

The king growled and moved on his bench. Then

he came forward and, stooping, loosed the High Smith's bounds. "It is well," the old nain said aloud. In his mind he said that in the brighter light the Orfas looked his full age indeed. Gray streaked the once yellow hair, now scanted. The smoothskin was no longer quite so smooth of skin at all: here wrinkled, there slack, elsewhere puffed with fat where not hollowed. It was nonetheless well, this act. Uur-tenokh-tenokh-guur sat and the king sat before him. Would he eat?—Would he drink? the king asked. The nain grunted, held his hand up. No. A silence fell.

"Listen," said the king at last. "What will you nains do when the barbar-folk invade?"

"I do not know that they will invade. I do not believe that they will invade. Why do you think so?"

The king restrained himself. Beneath his shag eyebrows his eyes looked at the nain like the waters of a wintry sea. "Why should they not invade? Are we now known to them as the source of great wealth? Amber and ivory and peltry—do they not value these things? Is there not a proverb, *When the prey stumbles, the hunter sharpens his knife*? They will invade to gain our wealth; they will invade because without iron, good iron for weapons, we are weak before them; they will invade because I tell you they intend to invade and it is in order to strengthen themselves by weakening us that they have cursed our iron—"

The old nain wheezed in the way that nains have and he said, "So now it is the barbar-folk who have cursed iron. And not the nains."

Slant-glanced, Orfas looked at him. "All the

witchery of iron is yours and you have kept it yours and we have suffered you to keep it yours. Besides the one kept by treaty at my court, there has been no forge outside of Nainland. If any man had a broken spear or plowpoint, he had to wait in hopes of a wandernain coming by with unbroken spear or plowpoint to trade him old for new plus a goodly gift. Nay, High Smith. I never begrudged the nainfee, myself paying highest of all. If this is at the bottom of all, let it be said the nainfee will be raised, let it be doubled, tripled—"

"It is not we."

The king's teeth clenched upon a strand of beard he had thrust into his mouth. "What has ever happened to iron without the nains causing it to happen?"

"This is a new thing, King. Had we not asked you long before you asked we?"

The king's hand made a movement, the king's face made a movement. The king was not in an instant persuaded. "You asked in order to cover yourself. But you have not covered yourself. Do you not know that *the king's ears are the longest ears in Thule?* I hear all things and I can, from what I hear, reckon all things. Thus it is that I know that iron is accursed, that the nainfolk have cursed it—at whose behest and for what purpose? Your silence is useless. Speak, then."

The old nain sighed.

"If you hear all things, then already you have heard of what the nains say among the nains in Nainland, namely that it is doubtless a device of the neglected wizards of Wizardland in order to ensure that they do not remain neglected: this curse, the death of iron. And if from what you hear you can reckon all things, then you can reckon what needs be done."

Now it was the king who sighed.

"You speak to me as though we were two old women pounding bark. You will speak differently if I come upon Nainland with all my men."

The old High Smith shook his massive head. "It is all one, if you come upon Nainland with all your men or with but one or none of your men. The forges of Nainland are cold, Orfas. The forges of Nainland are cold."

As he stepped from the outer to the inner of the two rooms in which he was to be lodged—or confined—he saw three great white flowers lying together upon a mat. He stopped still.

"I thought you might remember," a voice said. "I thought it might please you."

"Dame, I do remember," the old nain said. "And I am pleased."

Without bending down, he touched the flowers with his fingers. The blooms were scentless, but the room contained the scent of some that had never blossomed in the northern land of Thule. He had heard of the tiny horns and small flasks carven in strange designs upon strange stone, which contained the odorous essences of plants for which Thule had no name, delivered at intervals in trading vessels for great price and for the anointing and the pleasure of the Orfas Queen. He turned.

"Your face told me that you had never seen them before and that they pleased you; so I gave them to you, the three of them, and presently you gave me these—" She took from her broad bejeweled belt the ivory case containing the three small things so carefully wrought: dirk and spoon and comb. "Only see," she said, sorrowfully. The redrotted metal crumbled at her slight finger touch. "Can you not effect a cure?"

His broad stern face relaxed into something much like sorrow, he held both his hands straight up at the wrists. "They are so small," he said, musing. "All the witchery of iron known to the nains might just suffice to mend them. But the Orfas King would not believe that. If these could be cured, he would expect, he would demand, he would require, that all the rotting iron in his realm be cured. And this cannot be done. I do not say it can never be done. But it cannot be done now. I do not know when. Perhaps never again in our lives— Dame—perhaps never in our lives—"

A moment's silence. "I shall leave them at the forge," she said. Again a moment's silence. Her beauty seemed no less than it had been that long ago when Uur-tenokh-tenokh-guur had been a wandernain and she the lady of the Orfas Chief. He not yet king. She not yet queen. Sundry sayings floated in his mind. *One queen is every queen, every queen is all queens.* A beautiful woman, no doubt, and without question well versed in witchery, though he knew as little of queencraft as she of naincraft. She spoke again and said, "What have you to tell me of one who waits to return from across the all-circling sea?" He looked at her with pure unknowing and the certainty ebbed from her face. Then she said, "One who is not to be named, one who is the son of the half-brother—"

42

Understanding seemed to come not so much from his mind as from his broad and grizzled chest, whence a sigh of comprehension welled. "Ahhh. That one, who contested with— Nay, Dame, I haven't seen that one for four handfuls of seasons. Eh, must be full four. Nor heard of that one in that time. Say you that he has passed the all-circling seas?"

She gazed at him, a line between her brows. "Say you not? I see you seem full ignorant of what I had thought every nain, as every man, has heard: that one fled to the barbar-lands after fleeing court— when my Orfas gained the kingship—and has conspired to curse the iron so that, when he returns with hordes of barbar-folk, the kingsmen shall be as though unarmed. And say you that you know this not?"

He stretched forth both his long, long arms and held up both his thick and calloused palms— straight up—and he looked at her with pure unknowing.

Long he sat there alone, musing on what she had said, striving to make sense of it. Long he sat there, reflecting on old conflicts long forgotten— though clearly not forgotten by the Orfas King. Long he sat there, yearning for the red fires and the hot forges and the lust and joy of beating out the good red iron. Old forge songs and sayings came to him and old sayings not of the forge at all, such as *By what three things is a king made? By strength, by magic, and by fortune.*

Having set in the outercourt a watch of mandrakes who would shriek beshrew if so much as un-

43

bidden shadow fell, Merred-delfin, the principal witcherer, and the king and queen sat in the Room of Secret Counsel.

Said the queen, "What news?"

Said the king, "What help?"

Said the sage, "Much news, little help."

In his mind he said, *Little news, no help*. But one did not say such dire words, doom words, to the king. "Slayer of Spear Teeth, the Painted Men report a spy in the forest. I have no fear; the spy is dead."

Said the king, "Why dead? Why dead? From a dead spy no news can be gotten."

Said the queen, "Why not dead? A dead spy betrays no secrets."

Said the sage, "Great Dire Wolf, a dream has been dreamed of All-Caller, the great fey horn. No doubt this portends great good and who better to enjoy great good than thee, Great Dire Wolf?"

Said the king, "Ah."

Said the queen, "Oh."

Said the sage, "Woe."

Said the king and queen, "*What?*"

Said the sage quite swiftly, "Woe to the enemies of the King of Thule, the Slayer of Bull Mammonts, the Great Dire Wolf."

Said the sage quite slowly, "Wearing my Cloak of Night, I crept to the mines; there I heard the nain-thralls chanting in the Old Language, singing in the Magic Tongue. Lord and Lady, they intoned a tale of Fireborn, a thing of witchery of which they said it will cut good iron. *Good Iron!*—Lord and Lady! And if the nainfolk make words about a good iron, is this not a sign that the nains know

44

that iron will soon be as good as iron was before?"

Said the sage quite steadily, "Lady, you must use all your ways and wiles. Lady, you must prepare for many journeyings. Lady, you must wear many masks."

Then they set their heads even closer together and they whispered and nodded and bit their lips. The mandrakes muttered. And the shadows danced.

The breadth of the cavern was one nain wide and the height of the cavern was one nain high. Soldier guards, kingsmen, were obliged to stoop. More than once when the nain-thralls had been ordered to make the roof higher they expressed a gruff unwillingness to do so, saying that the roof would fall. So the guards were obliged to swing sideways the cudgels with which they struck the nain-thralls if the nains did not hack their stone-mattocks into the crumbly ironrock swiftly enough or if they lingered or stumbled while carrying the baskets of ore up the long incline and up the risky ladders set in shallow steps—up, up and up to the open sky inside the grim stockade.

Not long ago the notion of nain-thralls had only belonged to the past—a subject for winter tales or summer-night songs—how, in the days of bronze, when no king reigned, the nain-thralls dug the brazen-ore* and forged the brazen-tools; how the green-sickness came upon Thule and all bronze died and Chaos was king; how the nains discovered the secret witchery of iron and were free men at all times after, only paying the nainfee to the man king

* Although the presence of bronze as a crude earth is very rare, it is not unknown.

who in subduing the chiefs succeeded them as Power.

Thralldom was still—or rather, again—the subject of song and story.

But who cared what dirges the nains sang as they toiled or what accounts they told as they lay on their beds of bracken in their imprisoned nights?

The swans fly overhead
And the nains see them.
The moles tunnel through the earth
And the nains see them.
Stockades do not wall the swans
And the nains see them.
Fetters do not bind the moles
And the nains see them.

The baskets of ore were emptied into hand barrows and the thralls carried the barrows to the forge.

Once the nains were free as swans
And the nains see them.
Once the nains were free as moles
And the nains see them.

The forge was a flat rock rising from deep under the ground. The fire burned upon a hearth of other flat rocks, raised to a platform of the same height as the forge. The lumps of ironstone (and the articles of sick iron) were placed in the fire and burned. Although the kingsmen walked to and fro in violation of the ancient compact, which excluded them as it did all strangers, they learned nothing from their observations that did them any good. All ores looked alike to them; they did not know which ones to discard. All fired ironstones remained mysteries still to them; they knew not, though the nains did, which ones to discard as too brittle and which to pull out with greenwood toolsticks to be pounded upon the forge stone. Nor did they learn (or very much attempt to learn) the art of smiting with the stout stone hammer, turning and beating, beating and turning—all the while intoning in the Old Tongue:

> *Pound it, pound it, pound it well,*
> *Pound it well, well, well,*
> *Pound it well, pound it well,*
> *Pound it well, well, well ...*

because it was said, *The sound of the voice is good for the iron ...*

Perhaps it was no longer as good as it once had been. Nothing seemed to be. Day after day the nains toiled to make new iron, hacks and spears and knifeheads and arrow points. And day after day the productions of—at first—the previous year were returned to them, rotten with rust, flaking and powdering to be melted down and made new and whole again. The previous year, at first. Then the irons of the previous half-year. Then the previous season. Then last month, fortnight—last week.

One sweating nainsmith paused and pointed to a red-sick lancehead and his chest, thick and thicketed as some woodland hill, swelled as he spoke. "Not a seven-night since I beat this out—and now look how swift the iron-ill has afflicted it!" And he added in the witchery-tongue: "Thou art sick, thou art sick. Alas and woe to thee and us for thy very sickness."

And in his rumbling, echoing voice he began to chant and was joined by his thrall-fellows:

> Woe for the iron that is sick,
> > And the nains see it.
> Woe for the black stone whose red blood wastes,
> > And the nains see it.

He thrust the heap of rusted metal into the wood fire, deep, deep, till red coals and red metals met.

> Woe for the king whose men take captive,
> > And the nains see it.
> They take captive upon the paths,
> > And the nains see it.
> They lead away in heavy ropes,
> > And the nains see it.
> Captivity and toil lay waste the heart,
> > And the nains see it.
> Captivity and toil lay waste the flesh,
> > And the nains see it.
> The nain-thralls waste like iron,
> > The king's evil is like rust,
> The queen's lust is wasteful, evil,
> > Evil, evil, are these times,
> These days, consumed as though by wolves.
> When will the wolf confront the bear,
> > And the nains see it?

48

When will the stars throw down their spears,
*   And the nains see it?*
Confusion take these smooth of skin,
*   And the nains see it?*
When will the wizards' mouths be fed,
*   And the nains see it?*

The nainsmith seized a lump of iron and beat upon it with the stone hammer with great, resounding blows; and with each blow they all shouted a word:

When! Will! This! King-!-dom!
Rot! And! Rust!
And! The! Nains! See! It!

Chapter IV

Strange sounds he heard as he lay between earth and sky, rising and sinking, turning over and over again. Strange calls upon strange horns, strange voices, sounds. Pains, swift and passing like flashes of lightning, shot through him, again and again, then less often. The Painted Men were pursuing him; he hid from them; he hid in hollows beneath the roots of trees, he hid in the forks of the branches of trees, perched upon the crests of rocks, slid into the spaces between them. Always, always, saw the Painted Men prance by, panting in rage and shame that he had seen their naked skin. Always, always he stayed quite still. And always, always, they passed him by. And always, always they paused, legs frozen in mid-stride.

And always they turned, saw him; he felt the blows; all vanished.

Years went by.

When he became aware that he was returning to the everyday world he said in his mind that he would be very cunning and not reveal that he was no longer in the other world. He lay very still. Per- ~ps the Painted Men were uncertain if he were au. or dead and were lying in wait to see. He could not, through his parted eyelids, observe any- one or anything at all, save for the green network surrounding him and through which faint glints of sky were visible. But he had a faint yet firm feeling that if he were to roll his eyes just a bit to the right— He did not; he was too canny for that.

Besides, his right eye seemed swollen so much that—

And then a hand appeared, small as that of a large child, delicate as that of a young woman, yet not either: in the dim green light and through only one and a half eyes the hand seemed not entirely real, seemed almost translucent, had something about the bone structure, the nails—how many joints were there—nacreous as the inside of certain sea or river shells.

The hand placed something on his puffed eye, something cool and damp and soothing.

. . . and without awareness of intent to do so, he put up his hand and took the other by the wrist and sat up. Almost, he had not held the hand at all. Almost, it was as if his fingers were encircling something which had dimension without having substance—a delicate flower, as it might be, in the shape of a hand—and it slipped out from his grasp as simply as a sunbeam.

He had never seen a perry before.

Something slipped off his eye—he saw it was a dressing of bruised leaves and grasses, damp as though with the morning's dew: the perry's delicate and almost insubstantial hand took it and placed it on the swollen eye again and the perry's other hand took his hand, did not so much lift as guide it to hold the compress in place.

As the thin dew sparkling upon a cobweb, so did the perry's garments glint and sparkle; as the shy fawn stands in the gladey underbrush, not quite trembling and not quite looking at the intruder but poised for instant flight, so did the perry stand at the entrance to the leafy bower.

Arnten's body did not so much still pain him as it echoed faint reflections of remembered pain. Dim outlines of bruises he could see here and there upon his skin; he remembered enough lore of herbs and simples from his medicine-uncle to know that even the most puissant leaves or roots or grasses had not by themselves done all this work of healing: but the witchery of the perries, either intent or inherent or both, had aided them. At first he had had a fleeting thought that he might be in the hands of The Woman of the Woods, of whom many tales were told. To be sure, he had never seen the Woman of the Woods, just as he had never seen a perry—but his uncle had told him enough of each so that now he knew. His uncle who was his mother's uncle. His mother whom he had lost.

Arnten, find your father.

His father whom he had never had. The bear he could not find. The man, the mocker (had said Tall Roke) who had "gamed" his mother. The bogey for whom the boys of the village had held him slightly in awe and so much in scorn. Because of whom he had fled for very life. In which flight he had all but nearly lost his life. And now lay here, back from the edge of death, in the company of a creature far more fey than any nain, who spoke no word and barely looked at him and barely smiled yet had felt that deep concern for him and even now trembled between visibility and invisibility, substance and shadow, staying and leaving.

This gentle presence touched the cords which bound his pent misery and long-contained sorrow and did that which heavy and brutal blows had not and could not have done, and he covered his face with his hands and broke into tears.

He wept long and without restraint and when he had stopped at last, he knew it would be long, if ever, before he wept again. His eyes were wet and his chest ached, but these were slight shadows which would pass. All his body aches had gone. Something had changed in him forever. He dried his eyes, including the one ˀ longer swollen—and he was on his knees and ns. ˀ when he realized that the perry was no longer ther˷

He was aware of hunger and thirst, but more of thirst. He was aware of something else, a sound that had been sighing in his ears for as long as he had been in this shelter which somehow the perry had made for him. Sometimes the sound was as faint as a baby's breath; sometimes it grew almost as loud as the wind which carried it and sometimes louder, the rider overbearing the steed. Somewhere not so very far away was a river and now, in this moment of his great thirst (water perhaps needed to replenish that shed by his uncommon tears), great was the sound of its rushing.

The perry had stood upright, but Arnten found he was obliged to stoop, although certainly the grasses and the light, light withes would have yielded easily to his head. And so, while at the curiously woven opening, stooping slightly and about to go out, he became aware of two things lying almost concealed by the fragrant grasses of the shelter's floor. One was the witchery-bundle to which both bark basket and knife had been tied by deft and curious perry-knots; the other reappeared to him as though out of his dream-world between the time the Painted Man had beaten him to the ground and the time of his reawakening.

He recalled it now. When he had felt (and doubtless had indicated) thirst, something had glowed and glittered in the air before him, touched his lips and he had drunk. He had in his semi-thoughts believed it a fragment of a rainbow conveying the cooling rainwater to his lips; or a gigantically distended drop, suffused with multicolored lights, distilling into water on his lips and tongue. Now he saw it to be, less fantastically but not much less wondrously, a flask of some substance unfamiliar to him. Light passed into it and through it and he voiced wordless surprise on observing that he could see *through* it! What he saw was subject to a gross distortion. The flask was iridescent as the fingernails of the perry or the interior of certain shells, shining with a multitude of colors which shifted and changed. And it weighed much less than a vessel of earthenware of the same bulk. He marveled, but did not stop for long to do so; he placed it in the basket along with the witchery-bundle (knife again by hip); he considered what its name might be. For present identification alone he deemed to call it perryware.

And then he stepped outside, ready to seek his stream.

The sound of the river was quite strong outside the small grass shelter, shelter so slight that seemingly a fawn could have crushed it by rolling over, now that the protecting presence of the perry was withdrawn. He saw no traces of a fawn, but pausing a moment and wondering what had cropped the small measure of meadow, greenery and flowery, he saw the pellet droppings of the wild rams and—his eyes now opened—here a shred and there a fluff of their wool. His uncle had at one time amassed a small heap of their hooves (begged, doubtless, from hunters) which lay a long while in a corner, oily and strong-smelling. Once a nain had come to trade new iron for old and the rams' hooves had vanished—but for what consideration and for what purpose he had never asked and never learned.

The wind brought the river sound stronger, nearer, to his ears; the wind brought a scent of flowers, too. He was on a downward slope and in a moment, following the land contours, he found himself wading through the blossoms—first they were under his feet, then around his ankles; then they touched the calves of his legs, his knee—and he brushed them away from his face. Glancing at his hands, he saw blood.

Astonished, he looked around. Each clump of flowers grew from a fleshy green pod. Pod? Paw? There had been a wild catton in the village once, though not for long. Taking amiss being prodded with a stick as it lay stretching with paws outthrust, out from those paws it thrust its claws and struck—once—twice—at its tormentor. Who in one moment more had crushed its skull with a rock. So now, even as he half-halted his movements he saw a cluster of flowers dip down toward him, thrust out a sheaf of thorns and rake his chest with them. And then another. And then another. His arms, his legs, his back—he cried out, looked back, was struck again, flung his arms up before his eyes and staggered forward, raked with thorns and racked with pain. Then vinelets wrapped around his ankles—

And then, for a long moment, nothing.

Cautiously he opened his eyes. At once his ears seemed to open, too. There was a deep, intent humming in the air. He saw the thorn-paws of the thickets sway and waver. He saw them droop. He saw a swarm of bees spread out, circle; saw, one by one, the thorns draw back into their pods; saw the flowers open wider. Saw each bee select its first flower, mount and enter, heard the bumbledrone alter in pitch and quicken. Saw each plant stretch itself taut, then begin a slow undulant motion.

Saw himself utterly forgotten and ignored.

Once again had the wary feeling of being watched.

Saw nothing.

Made his way unvexed to the water, kneeled and drank.

Here the water rushed noisily over the rocks, there it eddied and circled silently into pools, out farther it glided with a joyful clamor along its main channel; then paused and murmured thoughtfully among the reeds. Everywhere it sparkled—in his cupped hands as he lifted it to his mouth, as it fell in droplets from his face, spun around sunken logs, made the reeds rustle. Something was trying to tell him—what? The reeds nodded.

Reeds.

With a movement so quick and unstudied that he sank one foot into water, he stood up, spun around and unslung his witchery-bundle—or, more exactly, the witchery-bundle supposedly left by his father—and spread out its contents in the sunshine. Fingers trembling, he unsheathed the knife and cut a fresh reed and laid it down beside the one in the bundle. Except that one was dry and one was fresh, they were identical.

Surely it was a sign.

The medicine objects restored to their coverings, he considered long what he should do. It seemed somehow natural that he should continue along the river; there, where he had found the first sign, might he not find at least a second?

At first he splattered along on the sand flats and gravel beds, the mudbanks and shallows of the shore. The river looked so wild, so wide, full of mystery (and, perhaps, menace). Here presently the salmon would come surging upstream, that was certain, but not now. What else might lie beneath those sounding waters was uncertain indeed. Sometimes the forest came right down to the brim and barm as though the trees would dip and drink. Sometimes he walked beneath towering banks and bluffs. After a while he saw the river divide and flow around an island, the main channel to the far side, the hither side forming a quiet pool, the shore of which was a sandy beach. On impulse he stopped, scooped out a hollow, placed into it his bundle and his basket with the perry thing, covered all with his leathern kilt, heaped sand over it. Then he turned and walked into the water.

The shallows had been sunwarmed, but now the deeper and cooler waters began to lap against his legs, higher and higher, and he saw and felt the flesh about each hair creep into a tiny mound. He saw that hair was now growing thicker about his man-parts. Abruptly, with a slight gasp, he slipped deliberately beneath the surface and for a moment squatted on the bottom like a frog. His breath heaved against his chest. He opened his eyes. All was strange in this new world. Then something was suddenly familiar; he opened his mouth and only the sudden burst of bubbles reminded him that water and not air was his surrounding. He surfaced, took another breath, slid down once more. In the curious light he exchanged quick glances with a small fish, then bent his eyes to the river bottom. Green light wavered in the green water and rippled over the green stones.

Reed in his medicine bag, reed beside the water.

Greenstone in his medicine bag, greenstones beneath the water.

It was the sought-for second sign.

The boy-frog squatted on the sand, sand clinging to him here and there, and looked at the other two small things in his budget of wonders: the beechnut and the bear claw. Certainly the last was the sign of the Bear himself, and by now it was plain that what the Bear was saying was, *Seek these others if you would seek me. Find these others and you will find me.* In the way a scout leaves signs along a trail so that those who follow may see and know what his message is, so the Bear had left these signs—not indeed in any sequence set apart by space—so that one who followed after might follow farther yet.

All clear, that. But what was the meaning of the beechnut? Beechnuts were good to eat, though perhaps not very good. The black swine of the woods were said to be fond of them. It wasn't clear what connection the wild swine had with the bear. Perhaps none. He began to feel confused and set his thoughts to tracing their way as though through a forest path: Bear—black swine—beechnut—well enough, by working backward he had come at least to some certain thing—beechnut—forest—trees—

Beechnuts, whatever else they indicated, certainly indicated a beech tree.

Not bothering to brush the sand from his bare legs and bottom, not from the leather kilt he swiftly and absently donned, he slung on his gear once more and set off along the river. But this time he walked along the dry land and looked, not down, but up. And so, by and by, by its silver-gray

58

bark and its pale green leaves, but most of all its height, he saw the trees he sought. Some long past storm or earthshake, or perhaps a hidden subsidence of the ground beneath its roots, had inclined it at a slight angle, for it was near enough the river for the stream in spate to have undercut and then covered up its excavating—or, perhaps the blow of a thunderstone had bent it; above the lowest branch, many times his own length high over his head a great scar was burned into the massive trunk.

Once again he had the feeling of being watched; the feeling ebbed again.

And there was certainly no sight nor sign of a bear.

His disappointment was great. It would have been easy to stumble or falter, only that day's morning had he gotten up from a daze of illness which had lasted—he realized he did not know for how long—and he had barely paused for rest. He had drunk once. He had not eaten. Weakness rose inside him. What had he expected? To find his father and, in finding him, an end to all mystery and aloneness forever? Had he expected to find a father sitting at the bottom of the huge beech tree, ready to welcome him with warm embrace? Here he was, Arnten, and he was as alone, as hungry, as unknowing as he had ever been.

What then was he to do? Slump behind the shelter of a bush and sleep and die? Weakness vanished. The very force of its sensation became a strength that blazed up within him and made itself felt without. He felt his skin tingle with something close to rage against this curious father who had cost his mother's life, had never come near to see what he had begotten, had left his cryptic messages with the nains alone. A father who might be dead, long dead.

Had he been pursuing a ghost? Had he himself perhaps died already under the blows of the Painted Man and was now himself but a ghost? Did ghosts hunger? He allowed himself a cry of anger and bafflement. Then, fiercely, he filled his bark basket with such nuts and berries and leaves and shoots of greenfood as were close to hand. At a small trickle on its way to join the stream, he filled the perryware flask, stopped its neck with a plug of fern. He arranged everything to hang behind him. Then, angry and hot-eyed, defiant and determined, he set his toes and fingers in the cracks and ridges of the beech tree's bark and began to climb. For the first time he allowed himself to speak his thoughts aloud.

"I will go up!" he said, through his set teeth. "I-will-go-up!" He inched up. And up. "And I *will* find out!" The bundle and basket dangled, swung out, bumped back, grew heavier. "And until I find out"—he panted, dug in once more, advanced, advanced—"I will not come down—"

He swung one leg over the lowermost branch, hoisted himself up, pressed his head to the rough bosom of the tree and hung on for very life against the wave of vertigo which threatened to plummet him to the ground. Slowly it passed and slowly he opened his eyes. The lazy wind swung into his face, laden with scents of the rich earth, of flowers and other growing things. He looked over leagues of land and the swelling and falling away of hills, the glittering serpentine length of the river, forest forever a great green roof. And far, far off, so distant that he could not be sure, he thought he saw thread-thin smoke. It might have been his village. He thrust forward his chin so suddenly that he felt a creak in his neck and, with all his force and might, spat in its direction. And then he allowed himself to realize that the lightning-burn upon the tree, just above the branch, was actually a tree-cave, a hollow.

It was, he considered (with a shiver), too small to harbor either tiger or leopard; it even lacked the reek of a bird's nest. Serpents would not go so high. Slowly, cautiously, he passed himself into it. Part of the bark still lay in place like a shell. And, patiently awaiting his discovery, wedged with splits of wood, protected from the worst assaults of the weather, was another hide-bound bag. Inside this was a box of carved wood. And in the box, padded with red-dyed fleece, was something that lay almost outside all his experience. Long he crouched in the dim light, half-afraid to touch it; then his fingers played over the intricate carvings. There was mammont-ivory and horn of wild ram, horn of elk; there was bear claw, there was—there were many things. Parts of it moved around, circle-wise, when he turned them. Parts moved up and down from holes, like little levers, when he touched them. Shapes of beasts and birds were carved into it. No man—nor nain—nor perry—had devised it. It was wizards' work, and wizardry of witchery alone. It was a witch-horn, so huge and adorned and complex it could only be *the* witch-horn. Could only be All-caller, the great fey horn.

Chapter V

See then, in the late rays of the afternoon sun, while the grea. ᵗ circle still throws heat before descending for its slo. journey through the Cavern Beneath The Earth w...ᵕⁿce it will rise again next morning, a small, a very small Something sticking out its head from the bole of the huge beech tree. After the head, an arm, at the end of the arm a hand and in the hand—what? It is needful to come closer. A shaggy boy, not quite a new young man, excitement and triumph and also fear upon its mold-smutched face. Carefully he holds the great horn in both his dirty hands. Carefully he examines it yet again, turning its turnable parts.

Ah. Ahah. So. Here is the bear claw, as like to the bear claw in his witchery-bundle to make one think they had come from the same bear-beast. As, perhaps, they had.

The boy's full lips protrude, compressed in thought. So—here is the bear carved in ivory upon the horn band. Surely it was meant to come in apposition to the bear claw. He takes a deep breath, fills his dusty cheeks, lifts the horn to his lips. His eyes roll, his nostrils distend.

And below upon the mossy ground, while the echoes of the great cry, part growl, part roar, still send the birds whirling about and the leaves quivering, something comes into the open glade around the beech tree. Something comes as though the thicket were mere fern grass. Something comes crashing, comes trampling, comes on all fours, comes walking upright. Stands, stopping. Peering this way and that. Paws and head swaying. Issues a cry, part roar, part growl. Part challenge, part question. Puzzled. Vexed. Brute. Bewildered.

Bear.

Bear.

Bear.

A moment passes, or does not pass; endures without end. Then the bear coughs, grunts, sighs, brushes at one ear. Gurgles deep within its shaggy chest. Ambles and shambles down to the river. Stands there without motion. Then makes gestures which no bear has ever before been seen to make— or so it seems to the watcher up high. Who has ever seen a bear take off its skin before? Who has ever seen a man inside a bear before? Who has ever seen a man stride into the water and leave an empty bearskin lying on the bank behind, gaping empty, eyeholes looking up, sightless, at the sky?

Has anyone—?

Arnten plucked up his talisman and, though it was the familiar-most of any object he had with him, he studied it as though he had never seen it before. Almost, for that matter, he had never seen a bear before. Perhaps he had seen live bears one or two times—dead ones, before they had been all skinned and dismembered for food and hide, several times. The carving did not seem to have changed. The bear was still certainly a bear—except that it still certainly had man's feet. He could not recall that he had ever observed the feet of living bears, these must have been concealed in grass or underbrush, or perhaps he had just not been looking; likelier he had had his eyes (as he crouched fearfully out of sight) on the paws of the fore-limbs, on the fearsome jaws. Perhaps *all* bears had man's feet. But then a clear picture came to him of the four paws of one dead bear, cut off for the pot—and all were *paws*, none truly feet. And yet, might it not be that bears, alive, had feet like men, and that these changed at death? As for the bear below? Truly, he had not noticed. He did not know.

Well, regardless, he knew what he had to do now.

He watched the man (formerly bear) swimming strongly in the water, bobbing under, emerging with hair all sleek, shaking his head, then resuming his swim, finally passing out of sight around a bend in the river. He would certainly be back. But Arnten was certain that he would not be back at once. Unencumbered by any burdens, all of which he left in the hollow, he climbed carefully down; he ran, eyes racing between three places—the ground, lest he stumble—the water, lest the man, returning, see him soon—the bearskin, lest—lest what? Lest, perhaps, and most horrifying by far, the empty skin somehow take on life and move, either toward or away from him. For a second it did indeed seem upon the point of doing so and he gasped in fright. But it was only the wind raising a worn corner.

He seized the skin and ran, flinging it across his

shoulder and feeling it on his back, bounding and bouncing. He could see it, feel it, thankfully he could not hear it, he had no desire or reason to taste it. He could smell it, though, and its reek was very strong, partly bear, partly man. All these things he perceived without being aware of concentrating on them. He concentrated first on getting out of sight of the water. And then he paused to think of what he should do next.

And, with a start, realized that he had already done something. Perhaps he should not have, perhaps he should return and undo it. But he knew he would not. That which he had so greatly desired, the one whom he had so straightly sought, the source of his being and his childhod's woe, man or bear or man bear or bear man, the witchery creature which had been his weakness and must now be his strength . . .

"I am afraid," he whispered.

True, That One In The Water clearly had desired to see him, had left a trail for him to follow perhaps not as clearly as if it had been blazed, as if it had consisted of traditional and familiar hunters' marks or patterns (but blazing and patterning were not intended to be other than open for all who could to read). And yet—and yet, *why* had he intended that his son should some day follow? How sure he had felt the son would follow, would meet the nains, would understand the messages bound up in the witchery-bundle: but this was for the moment beside the point and the point was: the bear man/man bear was power, and power, as much as it was to be desired, so much was it to be feared.

Presently something showed itself in the river,

moving against the current. Arms flashing in the declining sunlight. A figure came padding out of the water on a sandbar, moving as a bear does on all fours, but was not a bear; moved to the other end of the sandbar, where, motionless, it seemed to be staring into the water. A forelimb moved so fast that the motion could hardly be followed. Something flew out of the water, sparkled, fell. Twice more was the scene repeated before, now walking upright, a fish in each hand and one in the mouth, the figure walked through the water to the shore and shambled up the bank. Another, smaller figure, watching, trembled. The tall one was thickly built, with hair (now slicked down flat with water) so thick that almost the skin could be termed a pelt. It seemed that all the brightness of the sky of Thule, which had only an hour ago been evenly divided, was now moved and crowded to one side and that side so much brighter; while a blue dimness gathered on the other side. The birds began to fall silent. The air grew cool. Leisurely, the tall figure ambled up the slope and onto the bluff. The fish fell from its hands and mouth and it dropped backward so that it came to rest sitting down, legs straight out and arms crooked upright from the elbows. It gave a great roar of disbelief and rage. Then it rose and stabbed at the mossy ground and took up something in its hands.

The talisman, the wooden carving . . .

Then the head rose and scanned the bluff, the brush, the crowded arbor of the forest. Abrupt growls from the thick chest formed themselves into rage words.

"Where are you?

66

"Why have you done this?

"*Where is my skin?*"

A voice came from somewhere up above, from the thickening darkness. "I will not answer your questions till you have answered mine."

"Ask, then—"

And the other voice, a moment silent, wavering a bit, but not halting, said, "Who are you? Who am I? What is next?"

Appropriately the backlog of the fire had come from the great beech tree. "Long since, I have made fire, or eaten food cooked on it, or food with salt on it," said Arntat. His hands, however, seemed to have lost no skill. The fish had been deftly gutted, gilled and grilled. Salt, in a screw of barkrag, was still in Arnten's basket. "Salmon will be better," Arntat said, smacking his mouth at the thought, "but these are well enough." Sparks leaped, embers blackened, glowed again. Abruptly he swiveled and faced the boy. "You be thinking, 'Is it to hear talk of fish and fire that I've come this long way, waiting?' Eh? I see it by your face, 'tis so. Arnten. I have waited longer than you. Be patient."

And the boy was silent.

And his fullfather said, "The bear is in the blood and the bear may take you as the bear took me. At any time whilest life blood be in you the bear may take you, for the bear is in the blood. If it takes you not, and it may not take you, if it takes you not then 'twill take your son and if not you and not him then 'twill take your son's or daughter's son for sure. Let this be no burden. Fear it not. I've dabbled and dallied with a queen of love, and though 'twas joyous passion, yet 'twas nought compared to shambling 'mongst the new berries or finding honey in a tree or scooping forth first salmon, when I was gone a-bearing," his fullfather said.

And he said, "Bear's weird be better than man's weird and better than nain's weird. As a man I've been a chieftain high with lands and wealth—you may let your ears drop, 'tis nought to you *where* and nought to you *what's-my-name-then*. You were not made upon empty bear hide in lawful bedchamber, ah no, you were made when the bear was in the bearskin. My heritage to you is other than to my other ⸺⸺ ⸺ons. Heed and hear me now, Arnten. By my witchery-bundle and by my shadow, sons you make outside the bearskin be outside the bear-blood. But sons you make when you be a-bearing and be inside the bearskin, the blood of the bear be in them. And if the blood of the bear be in them, then not running water nor icy pools nor fire-hot springs can wash it out."

And the bear was silent.

Beechwood makes hard embers and hard embers make long fires. Long fires make long tales. Long they sat there in the scented night and Arntat talked and Arnten listened and learned. He learned that the shift and shape was truly not confined to man to bear, that other creatures indeed could pair, could couple, could double and shift.

> *Bee and salmon, wolf and bear,*
> *Tiger, lion, mole and hare . . .*

He learned of the slow growth of metals beneath the earth's skin and the formation of amber beneath the sea, how amber was one of the things of the perries, whereas metal was a thing of the nains. Once there was a metal called bronze but at length it grew green and sick and presently it died. Now there was iron.

"The sickness of iron is red," said Arnten, "and iron is dying." Red glints in the ashes. Reflections in the eyes of the watchers.

"Aye, eh," muttered Arntat. "The sickness of iron is red." He swung up his head and his hand gripped his son's. "What say thee, bear's boy? '*Iron is dying?*' What?"

That he, knowing so much, should not know this kept Arnten silent and astonished for several heart-beats. Then he saw pictures in his mind: one, one, then he saw things moving, heard the nain tell of years since "Bear" was by them seen. Arnten said, "You have been long inside the bearskin, then, and that long you've not seen iron?"

Still the hand gripping his did not move. "*Iron is dying?* True, true, many springtimes I have caught and killed the great salmon and many summer-times I have climbed for honey in the honey trees and in the rocky clefts. Many falltimes have I eaten the last of the frost-touched fruits and the sweet flesh of nuts. And many wintertimes have I felt the bearsleep come upon me and felt the numbness grow inside my head and sunk into the lair till the snows grow thinner. Aye. Eh. I can count the time only by counting your time. You are barely a man. And the last iron I had seen, the last iron I had thought of, I wrapped well the iron knifelet in my witchery-bundle and hid it well for thee. May it be sick?"

Arnten did not mind the grip upon his hand. He crouched against the crouching body of his fullfather. He rested on that puissant flesh which had made his own and which was now his present as well as his past. Defying mankind and beastkind and time and the night, he let himself recline against the great rough beast which was his father and he let his hand recline in that great rough paw. Quietly, almost drowsily he said, "That witchery-knife alone is not sick. But all other iron is sick." And he muttered, "The nains," and he muttered of the nains. And he sighed, "The king—" and he sighed words of the king. And almost he fell asleep, comforted by the rough, warm body and its rough and powerful smell. Then the body moved, releasing his hand, and a sound which was almost a cry and almost a groan rumbled and broke loose from that strong fatherbody by the embers.

"Iron!

"The nains!

"The king!"

Almost he flew awake. He slid down so that he might stand up. The day had been long and there was still much to talk about. The day had begun with the mammont hunt and he had run far and he had been hurt and nains and perries and Painted Men pursued him and he ran along the river and now the long long day was over and he had nevermore again to run to bolt to flee and *Iron! Sick iron! The wizards!* and *The King!* sounded their names in the darkness. And the embers slid down

70

because they were tired and the embers slipped beneath the ashes and the embers slept.

In the morning the embers were awake again and spitting and flaring at the meat that turned, spitted and smoking. Arntat was still crouched by the fire as though he had never left it and as though the meat had come at his bidding and obediently slipped out of its skin and onto the spit. Arntat yawned hugely and glanced at Arnten and it seemed as though his teeth were still the tushes and the fangs of Bear, his eyes still Bear's eyes so small and cunning and sharp, his blunt face still Bear's muzzle and his hairy hands with long thick nails— The yawn closed with a snap.

The man said, "There was the lone one of you?"

"The—"

"Sometimes a she kindles with twain. Or more. My get, by your dam—"

"Only me, as I ever heard. I never knew her. Uncle said she drowned. Was mad."

Arntat grunted. "It was time for it to be done and I was there and she was there and 'twas done, so. If not she, another. If not me, another. If not she and me, then not thee." He took the spit from its forks and rested the savory roast, dribbling, on the grass. "So. The lone one of you. Called me from my bearguise." He seized his son by his downy shoulders. "Hid from me my bearskin." Son resisted, wordlessly, was pressed down nonetheless. "Carried off with him my token. Found the nain. Found me. Called me from my bearguise. Stole away my bearskin. The lone one of you." Arnten was on his back, flat. "Am I to regret 'twasn't twins? Or be one of such enough?" The single hand

71

quivered the boy belly as one would a pup's. Then moved, one hand, two hands, tore the roasted meat apart, slapped a part still sizzling on the place the hand had been—boy leapt up, yelping, bared his teeth and began to eat.

Boy teeth shining sharp in quick-closed mouth. Boy hand rubbing belly. Boy snout smelling savory food. Boy cub by bear man, tearing meat from bone.

Still eating when father got up and strode off, he followed at quick pace, still holding his own unfinished portion. "Arn!" he said. "Arntat! Bearfather!"

Bearfather growled over his shoulder.

"The hide! The horn! The witchery-bundle! Shall I fetch?"

Arntat growled, "The hide? Leave it be. I'll go no more a-bearing for now. The horn? Leave it be. Rather than call wrong, call none for now. The witchery-bundle? As you want." And he melted into the shadows of the all-circling forest. Arnten followed, thinking and eating as he went. Claw and reed and stone and nut, he had read their message and read them rightly; he could part with them for now. The hide with its medicine signs he needed not now. For a moment he begrudged the knife, the good knife of good iron. He took a longing look at the slightly slant and towering beech tree, casting a long shadow in the morning sun as it had cast in the evening. They were all safe up there in the hollow of the hidey-hole. And there, safely, let them bide, then.

Still eating, he slipped after his father into the dappled surface of the forest.

Arntat did not precisely linger, he did not exactly dally, neither did he rush ahead with great speed, nor slink through the woods. Some sort of game was being played. For neither did Arnten go so fast as he might. It was the game, then, that each should generally hold the other in sight, but only generally. And sometimes the bigger one would suddenly hide himself and as suddenly reveal himself when the smaller paused to look around, then proceed as though he had not been hidden at all. Before long they had developed many aspects to this game and little tricks and presently they were again and again filled with silent laughter at each other. Through many a clearing and burn and along the paths they played their game, sometimes Arntat leaping along a fallen tree as lightly as a squirrel, at least once Arnten dropping several leaves before being realized and looked up at.

It lasted most of the morning and might have lasted much longer, but then Arnten, running noiselessly around a great lichen-studded boulder, ran full tilt into flesh which only in that first second he thought was his father's. A swift blow and an angry word undeceived him before his eyes did—he who had for all morning dropped even the memory of blows and angry words—and, as he tried to scramble to his feet, tried to turn his head to see who it was, tried to run away any which way (all these at once), someone grabbed his arm and twisted it. Only then did he cry out.

The man's face had the look of one who kicks a dog not to be rid of it but for the pleasure of kicking it. Then the face changed and the arm released him, raised its spear; the mouth that cursed him gave a

73

sick croak as something snapped which was not the spear. Arntat was there. Arntat was holding, embracing, Arntat was crushing. Ugly sounds of witless fright then, from this other's mouth. Blood gushing from that mouth. And then other men, many other men, spears and clubs and then ropes, Arntat down on one knee. Arntat releasing limp and bleeding body, Arntat clawing out for a grip upon another. Arnten biting, beating. Arntat down. Arntat growling, roaring. Men cursing as much in fright as wrath. Arntat down. Arntat suddenly silent, save for his breathing in the sudden silence. Arntat bound. Arnten, too.

And after some moments of gasping, recovering breath, slowing hearts, hissing of pain, someone said as though to a question none had heard, "I don't know—I don't know— Eh? Ah? Nains? *No!* Nor bears—"

Another voice. "We be the kingsmen. Let the king say *what.*" And others, others. "Aye! Ah! Let the king say what!"

Chapter VI

The red-sickness of all iron flamed into a plague. At first whispered, it was now said openly that the king himself had caught the evil and the ill. Indeed, it seemed to be so. Red blotches were seen about his face and hands and all his face and limbs and frame looked wasted and hollowed. His voice cracked and croaked. His hands shook. In the morning he groaned and staggered. In the late afternoons his eyes would roll up and his eyelids roll down and he folded his legs and lay where he happened to be, servants hastily bringing furs and fleeces and lifting him and settling him again. For the length of time it took for the shadow of the sun-staff to move over two stones the king lay as one dead. And in the late night hours he tended to enrage easily, to shout and strike out and to cast things.

But in the early and middle afternoon and in the early and middle night times he was as well as ever in those days he was well. As to the first of these periods, it was assumed he was passing well, for his voice could be heard talking—talking, not groaning, not yelling—and as for the second of these periods, it was then that he held such gatherings as he held and saw such outsiders as he saw. In the red light of the hearth all men may look reddened and the dancing shadows may make all men look gaunted.

But not all men hide themselves in daylight.

Day by day the couriers trouped in. Night by night the king himself would see them and let himself be seen by them and from them receive the tidings which he had, of course, already received; for did he not sit upon his stool or lie upon his pallet behind the reed curtain while the courier made report upon the other side? Tirlag-usak, grown stout and gray in his service as a first captain of the kingsmen, generally stood forth as the couriers came in, each with the strip of white bark cloth bound about his head, which even toddle-babes knew signified *I am the king's mouth and I am the*

*king's eyes and I am the king's ears. Delay me
not—and if I need aid, aid me.*

"Thirty-deer Hill," the courier might say. Or:
"Whalefish Point."

Tirlag-usak puts out his hand. "Tally," he says.
"Why so slow?"

The courier hands over the cut and carved piece
of wood. He pants to show how hard he has run. Of
late there had been increasingly less sham in this.
Tirlag-usak, of course, knows whence every one of
the couriers has come but he sees if the tally stick
fits the proper one from his own box.

"Report sightings," he directs. "Swiftly."

"Good omens from the flocks of birds," says the
courier. It would not do to report *No sighting*.

"Eat. Wash. Rest. Return after evening meal."

The courier retires, sweating but relieved. His
tongue may be the king's tongue but that need not
prevent its being cut.

Behind the reed curtain the king's lips writhe,
the king's hands move convulsively. The king's
face grows redder yet. The red-sickness increases
fast upon him. And the red-sickness increases fast
upon the iron. The courier has gone. Tirlag-usak
remains standing. From behind the reed curtain
comes an anguished whisper.

"Iron? *Iron?*"

"The ears of the king hear all things," says the
grizzled first captain. After just a breath, he says,
"The king already has heard that it is not better. It
is not even as it was." After three breaths should
come the groan or hiss which has come to mean
Go! but Tirlag-usak today, after only two breaths,
repeats, "The ears of the king hear all things." And

76

says further, "The king has already heard that ten of his men who went north in a search for nains have this day returned with captives."

"*Uhh?*"

"One great and one small, as the king already has heard. The eyes of the king have already seen them and it may be that the king's eyes have already recognized one of them as the king's kin to whom the king's mouth will speak more words."

Tirlag-usak had spoken somewhat more rapidly than usual. Now he waits for the space of many breaths and he hears each of these breaths from behind the reed curtain. But no question now comes from behind the reed curtain and what comes thence at last is a cry of such agony and terror and rage that almost the hand of Tirlag-usak touches the woven reed barrier—almost he stoops to lift it. But he hears other feet, other voices babble and whisper and shuffle and sigh. Then nothing. Then, only then, he departs.

Later, in the enclosure where they were penned, Arnten suddenly looked up. Arntat, his father, did not pause in his shambling and shuffling, shuffling and shambling, back and forth and back and forth, head waving like a snake's head from side to side. It seemed he did not share his son's thought, a sudden one which projected into the boy's mind a picture of the mandrakes dancing to the sound of the small drum in his old uncle's medicine hut. The recollection was so clear that the boy sat and watched it inside his head for some time.

Mered-delfin beat the small drum and his mandrakes, which were the mandrakes of the king and queen, danced their witchery-dance and Mered-delfin watched them from the corner of his eyes and the king and queen watched them full front. Every feeling moved across the king's face, none at all disturbed the face of the queen. The mandrakes moved and the mandrakes moved and they mimed and mimed and they danced. At first, coming forth from their carved wood chest, the mandrakes' motion kept time to the tune of the witchery-drumlet. But after a while and after Mered-delfin had sung to them and hummed to them and chanted to them, whistled and drummed to them, then the pattern of their moving changed. They led and Mered-delfin followed, his fingers and his palms straining to keep up with them, to maintain the proper tune and rhythm upon the drumhead made from the skin entire of a dwarf deer slain without bruise or blood.

At length, when they had begun to repeat themselves and no chantings or whistlings could prevail upon them to enact any new pattern, Mered-delfin drummed them back and dancing they went, throwing up their root-thin arms they danced backward upon their root-thin legs, and climbed back into their box at last and closed its lid upon them.

Thus the dancing mandrakes. As for the watching mandrakes, they remained in the outer court and would shriek, beshrew, if so much as an unbidden shadow fell. And there they muttered and watched.

The chief witcherer licked his mouth and wiped his arm across his sweat-slick face and quickly rolled his eyes. The other two were not looking at him. Swiftly he set his countenance into its accepted lines. He softly clicked his fingernail against the side of the drum. They looked up toward him.

"It is as we have seen, it is as I have said, they have enacted the lineaments of the dream and mimed for us the finding and sounding of All-Caller, the great fey horn—"

The king grimaced and showed his sharp teeth. As he leaned forward on his hands and arms he seemed to crouch on all fours. "And where, then," he asked, "is the great good which you said this dream portended for me?"

Mered-delfin parted his thin beard from lips and mouth and dared to grin. The very daring of the deed made the king draw back, somewhat relax the tenseness of his pose. Witch Mered thrust out his hand and arm and described a quarter-circle in the air and let the hand extend two fingers in a point. "Can it be that the sounding of All-Caller has lured from across the all-circling sea an enemy who is not to be named? And with him a son begat in treacherous exile? Lured them thence and it must be alone?"

His master's grimace grew into a snarl. His eyes blazed red. He seemed like a creature of the forest about to hurl itself from its den. He gave off the rank and bitter smell of denizen and den. "I shall kill them!" His voice rose into a howl. "I shall have them killed! They shall be killed for me and before me!" His tongue lolled out of his mouth. "Limbs broken"—the howl prolonged itself—"impaled—

"Slayer of Bull Mammonts—

"—flayed—

"Great Dire Wolf—

79

"—disemboweled—"

The last word hung upon the air. The Orfas panted. His sides heaved. He flung up his head and again he howled. In this howl there were no words, but it rang with a lust for vengeance long delayed. In his narrow pen Arntat heard it and stopped in his mindless pacing and hearkened to it and his arms moved slightly and he stood still. The nain-thralls heard it in their tunnels and turned their massy heads on their short necks. Servants heard it and shivered and tremored. Kingsmen felt flesh pucker and hair rise and let their eyes roll to each other, and almost they clean forgot the tales of the ill-struck king, cloistered and shabby and sick and old.

"The Orfas," they whispered to one another.

"The wolf! The wolf!

"King Orfas! Great Wolf! King Wolf!"

"—King Wolf—"

Long the wolf-king lay upon his side, panting, wet with sweat. Then he jerked his head and in two silent bounds Mered warlock was crouching at his head. Said the king, "Not kill him?"

Said the witcherer, "Not yet."

Said the wolf-king, "When, then?"

Said the sage, "When the curse is canceled. When iron is well."

The king said no word. His eyes rolled up and his lids rolled down. He nodded. He touched his sage's hand. His queen kneeled beside him and he touched her face. The words last spoken hung upon the air.

And the words unspoken, too.

Arnten and his father were allowed to toil together; one of the guards had said with a guffaw that the two of them were barely equal to one nain. Iron was the nains' heritage and though they had been used to it in all its workings at their own speed and though timed toil was inhospitable to them, still the nature of mining was not strange. But it was all strange, strange and fell, to Arntat and his son. Only the unswerving friendship of the nains and the fact of his and his son's being still together relieved the toil at all. And worse by far than the toil was the circumstance of bondage, of confinement, of life now being limited to a set series of motions within severely limited space. All thralldoms are one same thralldom. The unremitting labor of the toil, the unremitting oppression of the guards, the ill food, cramped space, uncleanliness, lack of hope, dull hatred, scanted sleep, infinite heaviness of spirit—are not these the features of all thralldoms?

"It is harder, Bear, for thee than we," the nains said. "The tunnel fits we as the hoodskin fits the pizzle."

"Then I stoop," he said. Stooped, grunted. "I have stooped before." But his eyes were sunken. And his forehead bruised and scabrous, for he did not always think to stoop, nor they to warn him.

And the nains said, "It is harder, Bear, for thee than we. We be used to the smell of iron dust and fire and have forgot the smell of grass and waterflows."

"Then I shall grow used to this and shall forget that other, too," he said. But he did not grow used to it, he often was coughing, and there was that in his eyes and on his face which seemed to show that he was not forgetting. And one night when the begrudged fire burned low and the older nains had begun to creep into their sleepy-holes and kick the crushed bracken-fern into a brief semblance of softness—at last, that night his voice burst loud with, "But I cannot forget! No! No! I cannot forget!"

The older nains crept out from their sleepy-holes, greasy-sided, fetid, close. They laid their hands on his, and on his knees and arms and legs, their huge and calloused hands. And a few did so to Arnten, who had crept close to his father; and the heavy nain-hands were light and gentle. "Since thee cannot forget, Bear, cease to try," they said. "And speak it out to we." And the Bear spoke.

Not—at first—of the free life of sun and stars, grass and waterflows, salmon hunts and honey thefts, of timeless days and world without walls. These all, it seemed, though well remembered in general, had become as it were a design bordered in dyed grasses around a basket rim—turn it, turn it, now faster, now slower, and see the same sequences following forever; man's mind no longer holding in differentiating recollection any one sequence from any other like it—so it seemed, when by and by his talk took up those days.

But he began with other days, when he was a man's child among other men's children, he one and Orfas another and Orfas a little older. Not much difference in age and little if any in status, even after both presently realized that Orfas was in a way an uncle—that Orfas' father was the other's

82

grandfather, the other's father Orfas' half-brother. Both playing and tumbling and chasing dogs in one familiar yard onto which opened (so it seemed) the doors of many houses, yet all of them family houses. In those days they were but two among many and each father had several sons and neither more of a rival to each other than either was to any others. All the sons and cousins and uncles of that age had cast their reed practice spears and awkwardly fletched their boy-arrows and went creeping and hunting in the mock forests of the great yard. The years had flown away like the wild swans fly away, yet never do the absent years return as do the absent swans.

Boys had grown to men, passed through ordeal and initiation, learned which was their witchery-beast, dreamed medicine dreams, had found women and knew the milk of life to be within them. The hunt had ceased to be play and often man had fought with man, not for proving or for pleasure but for very life; and some had taken life and some had lost it. Some of all that company of boykin had died young beneath the feet or claws or within the jaws of wild beasts or had been dragged down beneath the waves by waterkelpies or by fierce hippotames. Others had made themselves house-holders and gotten children while still barely bearded. Some had sought a name and fame by captaining pursuits of whalefish or were-whales, tree-tigers, or had gone north into the snows to hunt the wild leopard. One had been lured by the bewitchments of the Painted Men (whose skin must not be seen).

"There was a certain great tree whose wide-

83

spreading branches we all climbed as boys. It became our gathering place and remained so even when we were men and gathered there more seldom. But whenever we so returned, there we went and there we looked to meet with our comrades and our kin of our age. I had been away and gone a full handful of years, and I returned and sat beneath the tree upon a seat made by an out-thrust of rootburl. There I sat and long I sat and many passed but none were of our old company. And then came one whose shape I knew, whose walk I knew, even before I kenned his face.

"It was Orfas.

"He came and I remembered it was right that I should rise because he was my father's brother of the half-blood, and so we at some length stood and faced each other. He had the slight semblance of a smile on his face. For a while we said no word. And then I said, 'It seems, then, that of all, only we two remain in this corner of the Land of Thule.'

"And he said, 'It seems that this be one too many,' and although I did not deeply consider on his words, still, a particle of them must have touched upon a particle in me—at once I said, 'Then let us both be gone and let us make a compact and both be gone together.' We made our compact and prepared a boat and formed an alliance with others, gathered our gear and store and had the witcherers discover the best day to depart. South-south across the all-encircling sea we went, to the barbar-lands we made our course, sometimes along the coast and sometimes up the great rivers. Betimes we traded and betimes we sold the service of our swords and spears, fighting now for one town or tribe or chieftain, now for another; and betimes we shared the plunder-spoil or betimes we kept it all, as it had been agreed, or as it fell out. And then for a while we went a-roving and a-robbing as we would and as we willed, until the durance of our compact fell away to expire, and there was only a handful of day-sticks left in the tallybag. One of us had a dream to take a certain course with our three vessels (as by then they were) and reach on the third day an island all suitable for our needs, which was done, and the day we broke the third stick we made our landfall and the island was as had been seen."

Everyone has in his mind the image presented by story and by song, of all the troves and treasures piled in one great glittery heap, "dragon-high, dragon-bright, sparkling while its seekers fight—" but it is not always thus in fact, nor was it so this time.

Said he who had dreamed the dream, "Think it clearly for yourselves. Will he who lives alone to claim it be wanting to lug it all back to the ships again?" There was a burst of laughter in which was no sound of love or warmth. It was done so, that the wealth was divided between two ships, which were dismasted, and the third was broken up at once to make a deck for the complete vessel, which was a double-hulled raft of sorts with a single mast. Then each man set to sharpening his weapons and mostly he sat alone, with no more than now and then a sideways glance to estimate the strength or calculate the skill of another; and sometimes the other, on whom his direct look might fall had

85

been his near-comrade; and some seemed to repent greatly of this compact and to wish themselves away.

But only one would live to go away.

The fighting field was laid out and deeply trenched around, and then the lots were drawn to select the two for the first combat. Orfas drew one of the black pebbles and a younger man, often a singer of merry songs, drew the other. He sang no song now but muttered charms as they stepped to the center of the field, but Orfas did not open his mouth as they faced each other. Then all the rest shouted *Ho!* and in that instant Orfas spat in his opponent's eye and as he blinked, dumbstruck, Orfas rushed him from the side of that eye and with his axe he split through his collarbone. The man fell backward with a great croaking cry. Orfas kicked up the fallen one's kilt and again he spat, now upon his foe's manhood, saying, "That is for the wench you stole of me a two months' since!" and then he brought the axe down once again.

And went and took his rest across the trench until every other man should have fought once—and then he would again be subject to the lots.

Not every victor lived to draw a second lot.

"Now," said Arntat, "I had killed my man and had killed my second man. And as I sat resting and waiting I chanced to feel an eye strong upon me and I looked up and around and I saw that it was the eye of Orfas. It came to me that I had felt it heavy upon me before but had not fully thought about it. And now all at once I recollected what had been said that time we met after long apart, under the tree of meeting; I saying, *It seems that*

only we two remain, and he saying, *This be one too
many.* It came to me so late as then that he had
long hated me, and I suppose that inside me that
one particle must have returned his feeling or I
would not have answered as I did.

"Well! So be it! I knew then that we two would
be the last to stand upon our feet and fight for life
and for treasure, winner take all. It was our weird.
I do not know at what point in our lives he had begun to hate me—or why. Perhaps he himself did not
know it till he saw me there under the tree of meeting. Perhaps until then he had thought I would not
come back, that I was dead; it may be that the
deaths of others of our line had gradually or suddenly given him hope that he would be chief over
all our line—and, as our line has always been a line
high in Thule, he may have bethought him that he
might some day be highest of all in Thule.

"If I were not."

The fire barely lived at all. Then someone blew
briefly on the dull embers and someone placed an
armful of bracken on it. "Eh, ah, Bear," an older
nain said. "Well I remember when the old asking
began to be heard again. *By what three things is a
king made?* and answered, *By strength, by magic,
and by fortune.* He who paid the nain-fee then, I
shall say plain, was not the worst as ever paid it.
But even kings live not forever. And in all that
struggle which came. Bear, some say thee helped
the Orfas, he being near of kin. Some say thee be-
foed him and would have been king instead. I ask
not and care I not. Thee has ever been the friend
of nains, as nains have ever been the friends of

thee. The Orfas winned the kingship and was made king as kings be made and he paid the nain-fee— *then*—full and fair. But the nains be feed to work in iron, not to set snares for bears—or men. We saw thee in the wildwood dwelling where never manfolk dwell at all, we told it to each other and we told it to the forge, but never did we tell it to the king."

"I know."

"Such rewards he offered, and such afflictions he threatened as never did we hear before."

"I know."

"That bitter winter when the birds fell frozen from the sky and the all-circling sea itself was turned to ice, far as ever eye could see, when no track nor trace could be concealed upon the snowy ground and no snow fell more from the fast frozen sky, then the Orfas came for thee, for Witch Mered did plot it out for him."

"I know."

"Corby Mered. Mered Crow."

"His witcheries espied thee out, we knew and said nought, he saw and said all. With many troops of men they came for thee, and circled around where thee had gone. Where could thee hide? We thought it woe, we whispered low, we told it to the forge, but nains mix not in the affairs of manfolk— would that man would mix as little in the life of nainfolk! They circled all about where thee had gone, they scanned the still, unbroken snow, they drew their lines inward as wading fishermen draw their nets, they met face to face and arm to arm in the center; but *Arn* they never met."

"I know."

He said, "I know. I know." Crouching in the

88

darkness marred by feeble flicks of flames, he said, "I cannot forget." A prisoner, he remembered himself a fugitive; though it had seemed bitter then, now long later it revealed its sweetnesses. And he could not forget.

The nains sighed and they sighed for him, not for themselves. The king had sought him then and found him not, and hunted him again and found him not. King and kingsmen hunted a man, but he whom they hunted was a man no more. He had become a bear.

Chapter VII

Day followed day and toil followed toil and slowly the great rust increased. Its pace was not steady. At times it had seemed to leap onward like a dread grass fire in the dry season, at times it had seemed to pause as though tired. Now for some long while, the red-sickness had gone at so slow a step that some did not perceive that it still continued until, perhaps, an axhead crumbled as it met the wood it could not cleave, or an arrowhead collapsed into a pinch of russet dust when the quiver was moved. And many still had not realized that the pest pursued its course.

But the king was not among the many.

It was not only that he asked or caused to be asked, "How goes it with iron?" of those who came from far off. He asked always, in hope of hearing what he would hear; but he was not content only to ask. The king had great store of iron, not in the armories alone, but in his own chambers, very near to him. Several times a day, if he did not go to iron things, he had iron things come to him. He looked, he tested, poked, probed, he scraped iron with his fingernails and he scaled with instruments which were not of iron. The king knew the rate each day at which the plague pursued. He knew it and he sickened from his knowing.

"Will you not leave off?" the queen asked him with a sigh.

"How can I?" he asked, with a sick and sidelong look.

There was almost a proverb in those days: *The queen grows not old.* Some had grown up hearing it and thought it a saying applied to all queens; that women who held the queenly seat, by virtue of the power of that office did not age. But in truth it was a saying which had not been heard before—although likely enough that any woman spared the labors of hoeing and bark-beating and preparing hides and all such toilsome work, who had but to put on her clothes and jewelry and suckle her children (and sometimes not even such slight, light tasks as that) likely enough that thus a woman, queen or not, would not grow old so soon and certain as the generality of her sex.

Still, the saying was a new one, as sayings go. Here lies the truth: quite early had her hair turned the color of a winter's sky, quite early and quite suddenly. Therefore most of Thule became aware of her when she in some measure already wore the mantle of more years than she had. And also her manner had already become grave and withdrawn.

90

Since the mass of folk did not observe her slowly losing what were common tokens of youth, gradually the saying came to be heard: *The queen grows not old*.

Some held this to be due to her command of witchery-wisdom. Only a few, and they not often and never openly, were lately beginning to whisper that she sipped the cup of the king's own years, that she stayed one age while he aged swiftly. And at least the very last part of this was true.

"You can leave off by leaving off." she said. Only a very few lines were to be seen upon her face—about the eyes, and about the corners of the mouth—but none at all upon her upper lip. "Rest upon your cot or couch and let others examine iron while you watch. And watch not too closely, that is to say, too nearly. Iron is sorely ill. And you are not too well."

A slight snarl moved his mouth, but did not move it much; his next words and the inclination of his head showed how little the snarl was meant for her. "You are ever gentle of me in word and deed—but I know well what they say out *there*—that I have caught the iron-rot. Perhaps I have. But if I have caught it, I have it—so what good then be distance? Or any precaution?" He moved nonetheless to his couch. Muttered, "If iron die, then I die. If I die, let iron die. But let we not die, either, nor the barbar folk come swarming—savages from over the circling sea—" He let himself down on his couch and leaned on the pile of prime pelts sewn in bags and stuffed with the downy breast feathers of swans. His eyes were sunken and closed. A long breath shuddered and sighed in his throat and fluttered his cracked and blistered lips.

Suddenly his eyes flew open. Those of the queen were fixed upon his. "Why do you think he came back alone? Or did he?" Without giving her time to reply he rolled his head back and forth and clenched his hands. "Only because Mered-delfin feels that this traitor may somehow prove the key to the cure of iron do I spare his life." His teeth showed and sounded. "I should never have spared it before." Another thought worked its way across his ravaged face and the queen drew near and kneeled beside him. "Mered-delfin—he said that you must prepare to wear many masks and to make many journeys." She gave a slow, single nod. The king said, "Wear one mask now. Make one short journey."

From time to time word came, presumably from the king, to switch the mining from the open pit to the tunnels or from the tunnels to the open pit. Evidently neither change had perceptibly improved the fate of iron, but from time to time still came directions—*Change.*

Thus on this day the mattocks swung up and down upon the encircling path which went around and around about the great deep pit, up from its narrow center to its wider rim, digging deeper into the walls of ruddy ore. *Up* the tools went, paused, still scattering dust; *down* they fell, a grunt, a thud, and some were of bone and some were of stone, but none were of iron. Arnten had been detailed to carry the yoke with its brace of leathern water buckets and a drinking horn slung about his neck on a thong. For the most part he kept his eyes on the uneven footing of the circling path, but when he paused to allow one of the nain-thralls to drink he allowed himself to look up. The yoke had bitten into his flesh, but he preferred it out here in the open pit. He thought they all must. It was like being inside a great clay pot, one only partly made; the pot-woman had rolled the strip of red clay between her palms and coiled it into the rough shape of the pot-to-be, but she had not yet taken up her shell or shard to smooth it. The pit was like a great clay pot and they were inside it, small as mandrakes.

Of course, pots had no light blue lids on them. Against the rim, outlined, stood the guards. His eyes swung around. The nain groaned gratefully between gulps. All about the rim the guards stood at equal intervals, weapons sticking up like fishnet sticks. But at one place there were a number of them grouped together. They moved and he saw that one of them had no spear, no club, seemed to be dressed differently. Dressed more.

The nain gave one last groan, looked enviously at the rest of the water in the pails, licked his mouth and bristles and put the flat of his huge hand between the boy's shoulders below the yoke the nain had effortlessly lifted into place, gently shoved him on his way. The yoke grew lighter as he went from nain to nain. Presently he stood before his father. Arntat looked at him a moment with a dull gaze. His eyes were filmy. Then they saw the boy. A faint smile rested briefly on his haggard face. Suddenly the boy cried out, "I am sorry! I am sorry, Father, that I ever took away the bearskin!"

The yoke was lifted, the buckets put down. "I had set all things to *that* end," his father said. "As for all *this*—it be our weird. Ah, water. Good." He took the horn and dipped it full and raised his head as he raised the horn to his mouth and his eyes settled on something beyond. For a moment he did not move. Then his teeth clicked and rattled on the rim of the horn. Then he made sounds in his throat. And next he drank. But his eyes never moved.

A guard, perhaps thinking that they had been too long over the matter, approached—the expression on his face was part sneer and part fear. He gave a quick look over his shoulder and with his head motioned to another guard to follow. This first guard set his features for stern speech and gave the hand which held the club a shake or two. But what he was about to say went unsaid, as from above and beyond, a voice whose syllables the boy could not make out came floating on the air and echoed twice or more. The guard's face twisted in his own effort to comprehend, then showed surprise —regret—relief. The guard turned away, turned back, spoke to the guard behind. And this one gave a quick look at the captive father and son, a quick look up and beyond. He shrugged. The two king's men moved apart and drew themselves up in a stance of bravado and watchfulness.

Arntat let out a long breath. One hand groped for his son. The other then hung the horn-thong around the boy's neck. A drop of water trickled from it, made a muddy wormtrack through the dust on his chest. Both hands found the yoke and lifted it as the boy bent to receive it. Both hands

94

turned the boy around and told him, plain as
words, to be on his way. Arnten went. He went
several steps. He heard behind him the grunt and
the thud as, rest over, toil returned to, the mattock
struck the red-ore ground. Then he stopped and
looked up, whither his father had looked, up to
where the guards had looked. Nothing was there.
His eyes, darting about, saw again the group of
guards. They had just begun crossing over the rim
and, as one by one they stepped out of sight, he
saw once more the unarmed person among them,
who paused upon the edge between earth and sky.
Pausing for a moment and looking back, this person for an instant seemed to have raised wings
poised for flight.

Wide-cut sleeves. A woman.

She vanished over the rim.

A blow caught him in the ribs, a rock fell and
bounced. He dodged the second. It came from the
guard who had desisted from striking him and his
father before. But he had to move and turn his
back and yet balance the yoke and the buckets, so
he could not run. The third stone caught him. And
so did the fourth.

When the thralls lay down their mattocks and
began to load the broken ore into the barrows the
first captain looked, saying nothing. Afterward he
gestured to Arnten and Arntat. "You two—or you
one and half"—the guards guffawed—"take the
tools to the tunnel. The rest of you to the forge."
Two by two, the nains stooped and took up the bar-
row poles. Low at first like a mutter, then a rumble,
as though the voices had descended from mouth to

throat and chest; then so very high it seemed almost that they sang not at all as they padded along the curving path; and then cry after cry, as great wave after great wave breaking upon the rocks—

> *The swans fly overhead*
> *And the nains see them.*
> *The moles tunnel through the earth*
> *And the nains see them.*

The guards could not ken the words, but the sound of the chant made them uneasy. They howled and mocked, they threw stones, small ones but vicious and thrown hard.

> *The king's fire gives no light,*
> *The queen's light gives no fire,*
> *Evil, evil, are these times,*
> *These carrion times, consumed by crows.*
> *When will the wizards' mouths be fed.*
> *And the nains see it?*

The tools were gathered and bundled together like great faggots of firewood. Father and son bowed their backs beneath their loads and turned their faces toward the tunnel. It was not the load that made Arntat tremble now, nor was it his last labor of the day that made him sweat and gasp. Unwilling, unwilling, slow, were his steps and he craned his neck at the darkening sky as though he would never see it again.

Beyond them the guards seemed to have been taken by a frenzy, stoning the nains and shouting and feinting at them with clubs and spears. But above all such noise the wild chant continued to be heard.

The king's evil rots like rust,
And the nains see it.
When will the stars throw down their spears,
And the nains see it.
Then may this kingdom turn to dust,
And the nains see it.

Sometimes the bigger Arn trudged back and forth in the tunnel, head stooped low—perhaps for safety, perhaps from apathy—hands against the sides as though at any moment he might push one or another of them aside. Sometimes he shambled on all his limbs, head weaving from side to side. But he was sitting motionless when the dry bracken rustled as it sometimes did, as though remembering when it was alive and yielding to each slight breeze. And a woman came in. She first saw the smaller Arn, and for just a moment the smooth composure of her face was disturbed—how curious, then, her expression! He moved at once to his father's side and her face was as before. In a single motion, effortless, graceful, she seated herself, her legs tucked under, her hands resting in her lap. Son looked at father and he thought his father looked as though he had always been looking at her.

"Yet another son gotten, Ahaz-mazra," she said. "And so much younger than the others." She made a slight sound as if pleasantly relaxing from some not too onerous task and she said, "You will want to know about your other sons."

Lips barely moving, he said, "Either they died or they made their peace. I can do them no good. Nor they me."

Calmly: "You may do good for this one then," she said.

This one, crouching next to his father, was not much thinking how good could be done for him. Part of his mind was entranced by the appearance of her. Part of his mind scurried and searched, as a squirrel rousting nuts, for certain words his father had said—when? Long, long ago. When they were free.

'Tis nought to you what's my-name-then. But now he knew, his fullfather's name then was Ahaz-mazra and if this woman knew it she had known him then. Her underdress, beneath which her feet were tucked, was all of blue. He had never seen so much cloth of blue before, blue was a precious color, a sky color, and he had heard more than one say that far-far-away at the farthermost edge of the world dwelt the Sky Gatherers and that all the blue in the world came from them, scarce, scarce, precious and beautiful blue: but his old uncle had said this was in no way true and that blue was made from an herb called woad; it did not flourish in Thule, was brought from the barbar-lands and traded for amber, weight for weight.

Ahaz-mazra. And not Arn.

My other begotten sons ... made upon empty bearhide in lawful bedchamber. Her sleeveless overdress was the whitest white he had ever seen, paler than the common pallor of barkcloth, and came to her knees. Round yoke and hem were broad and complex broider-work in several colors,

flowers and leaves and thicket—something else
which he could not quite determine and which
peered out of the thicket. Around her neck was a
rope of pieces of amber wrapped in golden wire.
Her face was strong, serious, totally self-assured.
Although she had come from the free, the outside
world, she had come neither to triumph nor to con-
descend. *I have dabbled.* Why was that word in his
mind? ... *have dabbled* ... Or should it be *dappled?* That made no sense. Yet the memory that
went with the words was of his father's face dappled by leaf shadows as he held for a passing moment a branch he presently threw upon the fire. *I
have—*

"I have done ill enough for him by getting him,"
said his father now to the strange woman. Who
said a strange, strange thing indeed.

"You may get him back with you whither you
both came—on a ship already prepared in all
things—at dawn tide three days hence," she said.
"You have only to renounce the curse on iron and
to swear by your shadow and by his that it shall
stay renounced. And you may even delay compli-
ance to the last—when the third day's sun comes up
and shadows first appear—upon the very shore beside the ship."

The sick, confused look, which had been absent
since her entrance, now returned to the man's face.
He muttered, uncertainly, "The third day's sun?"

"It is three days' journey to where the boats
are."

He squinted, trying to resolve all into sense.
Then he in one swift rush was on his feet and
Arnten cried out and put his hands on his own head

99

as though feeling the pain of his father's crash into the tunnel top. But one or two fingers' breadth away, the man's head stayed, stooped. The woman had not moved. She did not even raise her eyes. And the man fell to a charging position, his eyes level with hers, his face very close to hers, his eyes now suffused with blood.

"Innahat—erex," he cried, "ah, eh! Does that crow still live, that he has stolen all the wits of thee? 'Wither we both came?' 'By ship?' 'Renounce the curse on iron?' What babblement is this? From nowhere did we come by ship! No word of any curse on iron heard I ever till my cub here did mention it, before we fell into the nets of your long-tongued lord! 'Swear by my shadow and by his?' Eh, ah! By my shadow and by his, then—"

More than once, after having returned in from out, Arnten had felt sickened and dizzied. The sun might have been the cause, beating as it did on him all day. Such a moment came upon him suddenly as he wondered what great oath his father was about to swear upon their twain shadows. He closed his eyes. He did not hear if the oath were sworn. He did hear the distant droning of the nains as they returned, as their voices rose suddenly and dropped again. The strange woman was now gone, he saw. He saw his father's eyes were fixed on his and all manner of strange things he saw in them.

"Eh, ah, Bear! What odd thing we seed by yonder tunnel-mouth but two, or three! Howt did leap! A hare! Was't an omen, eh?"

"I ken't not, if omen 'tiz," another nain said. "But 'twas as thee say, senior Aar-heved-heved-aar,

a great puss-longears indeed, and would I'd a snare
to catch she doe-hare, do she return—eh?—cub?"

For this other nain looked now at Arnten, who
had stood up, although still dizzied, waving his
hand, trying frantically to put a thought into
words before the thought fled. "The hare came in!"
he said, almost stammering. "The hare came in!
What way she came in, would she not go out?"

The man put an arm around his son. The com-
forting nain-drone and nain musk surrounded
them. The boy's head drooped upon his father's
side. He felt weak and sore and hungry. Food
would come. Words sang in his head and faint fires
danced there. *Bee and salmon, wolf and bear.* A
rough hand rested gently on him. *Tiger, lion, mole
and hare.*

Fetters do not bind the moles.
And the nains see them.

Chapter VIII

Aar-heved-heved-aar that night sent a youngster
nain to search out the passage where the hare had
run. Guards did not trust the lower levels at night,
would not even if the nains were gone. Posts and
watch fires were at pit mouth only. Even wind and
rain could not drive the guards more than a few
feet inside after full dark. The nain-senior knew
this, but did not trust the slickskins as cowards any
more than he trusted them as braves; he chose to
lessen all risks. It was not true that nains had full

vision in the dark, but in this wise their eyes were in between those of men and those of beasts. The younger nain reported that although the tunnel appeared to be a blind gut, yet it did not end clean. A huge pile of debris at one end seemed to show that it might not always have been a blind gut—that perhaps the roof had fallen in at one time. And, more than this, the younger nain had sought and found the scent of the hare and it had seemed to go on up the pile of detritus to its peak.

"But I clambered not after it," he concluded.

"Wisely," said the senior. "For though I be as much a-zeal as any to be gone from here, needless risks we must not take. It is man who is impetuous, but we nains do be deliberate, so—"

"Feed the wizards."

Aar-heved-heved-aar, true to his penultimate word, reflected. Then, "Eh, ah, Bear. Say thee well."

"Feed the wizards!"

The nain-senior looked up at the man—for all his breadth, the nain was no taller than Arnten—and nodded his massive head. "That must be our aim, hard task though it be. It is the coming death of iron which has turned this king's head mad and turned his hands against us all. His need be great. But is our need not greater? If he do die tonight and tomorrow we be told that we be free, what then? Iron be our life, without iron we be dead nains. 'Tiz but the first step, getting gone from here. He will pursue we, but if he should not, what, eh? We do make the hoe, but we hoe not; we have traded iron and iron's work for most our food. We make the spearhead, but we cast no spear. And if

102

we will to eat in the woods, as the wild brawnes do —say, ah!—be not the wild brawnes a fitter match for us, be we not armed with iron?"

He uttered a long, shuddering cry and his head shook so from side to side that his thick hair rustled upon his broad and shaggy shoulders. "Men gender much," he said, "and the men-wives bear often. Nains gender seldom for our passion be for the forge and few are the nain-brains our shes do get. Before the Great Bear took starfire and gave it we and beteached we how to delve and deliver metal from the earth's belly and to mold and shape it as the bears do mold and shape their cubs—before even the yore-tide—men were few and nains were few and lived they twain folk far apart, for broad and long be Thule.

"But since then men have swarmed—yet the nain's numbers do stay the same. Still be Nainland far from menland, eh but ah, *it be not so far as once 'twas!* Men can hunt without iron, men can farm without iron, men can still beget them many mennikins without iron; men can do without iron and I betell thee this: *If men may live without iron, men may live without nains.*"

The echo of his voice was long in his listeners' minds.

He divided them into nine watches and to each watch he assigned a third part of one night. And the first watch for the first third of the first night began at once to clear away with slow care the rubble at the end of what they had begun to call the Doe-Hare's Den. The nains stripped off their leather kilts and piled loose stone therein, then gathered up the corners four and slung the juried bags over their shoulders and trudged away on noiseless feet to empty their loads well out of sight in yet another disused corridor. And then to return. Thus, while the work went on, none lost more rest than one-third of every third night; and, after many nights, the toilers in the Doe-Hare's Den, pausing a moment for rest, recognized in their nostrils the bitter, faint, familiar smell of woodsmoke—and recognized that an aperture, of whatsoever a nature, existed between them in their captivity and the unfettered outside world.

And thus the elusive memory returned to the boy Remembering woodsmoke and firelight and father's words, he said, "The strange woman who was here. Was she the queen of love with whom you dabbled and dallied?"

A silence. "Eh, she was."

"Be that why the king do hate thee?"

A growl. "She said he never knew."

"Then why *do* he hate thee?"

A grunt. "Has thee forgot my tale of how he and me vowed a compact and at the end stood face to face to fight for treasure and for life, winner take all?"

"No, I remember that."

A cough. A second, longer, deeper cough. A gasp. "I won. He lay at my feet. He groveled and gibbered. I raised him up, gave him half the plunder and I spared his life. That is why. For this he cannot forgive me."

In the darkness he heard droning of dry and dusty voices and he knew it was the wizards that he heard. He heard them droning as though ineffably bored and weary, as though repeating over and over to themselves, lest they forget, forcing their dust-choked voices and thinking with dust-choked minds, at a great distance away, repeating something of great importance which must not be forgotten—*The Bear dies, iron dies. The Bear dies, iron dies. As the Bear comes to life, so must iron come to life. As the Bear comes to life, so must iron come to life.* A pause, a faint gasp, the click of voices in dry, dusty throats. And again and again the droning recommenced. *The Bear sleeps in the ground, so must iron sleep in the ground. As the Bear sleeps its death-sleep-life, so must iron . . .*

The Bear dies, iron dies . . .

Endlessly he heard this. The sound ebbed and faded away as he felt himself gently rocked.

"*What?*"

"Bear's boy, it be time."

Time for iron, time for . . . But the droning voices were away and gone. Had he heard them echoing thinly in a cavern somewhere? Or was it only the familiar echo of the nain voices in the mine? Confused, already forgetting, he got up.

Still half-asleep he followed, sometimes stumbling, as the men filed from their sleeping-cell into unguarded tunnels. In the Doe-Hare's Den he saw the now familiar sight of and heard the now familiar sounds of debris and detritus being shoveled and scraped into the carrying-skins. But while this still went on he heard those who watched and who waited discussing whither they should go when they had made their escape from the mines: and should they go in one body for defense, or should they split up and make their several—or it might be their many—ways, in order to divide and so to weaken their pursuers.

He did not hear if an answer had been concluded, let alone what it was, for Aar-heved-heved-aar took hold of him and said, "Bear's boy, 'tis thought they have broken through up ahead. Get thee up then, for thee be but small as compare to us and maybe can find out—"

The senior nain did not finish his phrase, but propelled Arnten forward, saying, "Up, then, and up and up."

Though so much diminished, still the pile was high and required climbing. He half scuttled and he half slid as he set to climbing. And he had somehow a fear that, though he went on his way slow enough, still, he might strike his head there in the darkness; and from this fear he went slower. And every few paces he paused and thrust his hands forward.

And by and by he felt his hand as it scraped the face of the cavern suddenly fall through into nothingness, and he fell forward a bit and he grunted rather than cried out. And ahead of him, where yet he could not see, ahead of him in the black, black, blackness, something moved which was even blacker (though how he knew this he did not know). Something made a sudden movement and a sudden noise and he had the impression that something had been waiting and hearkening, listening very closely, he had an impression of a head cocked to one side—

And before he himself could do more, the sound from the other side of the hole ceased to be startled, flurried, resolved itself into the flap of wings in the darkness.

And he and all of them heard the sudden sharp cry of a crow. And again, farther away. And once more, faint.

Now the work quickened, concentrated and focused on enlarging the opening. An opening onto the world at large? Or into another cave? If the latter, still, this next cave must itself open onto the world at large, else how came any bird to be there? But the stone or bone blades of their picks no longer sank into rubble. Either they sprang back as they were swung against the lips of the scrape-hole or they shattered. The nains began to mutter. Then Arn came forward on all fours, reached out his long, shaggy arms, felt and pawed and groped in the darkness.

"It seems that two slabs of rock all but meet face to face here," he said. "Some bit of softer stone did rest between them, as might a piece of stale bread between a dead man's teeth—

"Now, part of that had weathered away, else that hare had neither entered nor left—and we have battered away the rest—but the teeth be fixed firm. Somehow we must crack the jawbones, then. So—"

His voice fell into a muttering growl. "We must break the jaws of the rock," he said once more. "How?" he muttered. "How? *How?*"

A dull glow from a brazier of coals made shadows as the king moved slowly and painfully upon his bed. Something scuttled outside the chamber. Someone entered on hands and knees. The king lifted his head, stopped, groaned, rubbed his face, moaned.

"You smell of mold and of trees," he whispered. "Well—what?"

Mered-delfin panted a moment. Then: "Slayer of—"

The king made a noise of loathing, deep in his throat.

"Damn all fulsome phrases! None's here now save thee and me. *What?*"

"Wolf—the mine-thralls—trying to break—" His wind failed, his voice caught in his scrannel chest and throat.

His master finished the words. "To break out? Eh? To—" He struggled up, hissed his pain, rested on his elbows. Raised his voice. "*Hoy!*" he cried. "The captain of the guard! *Hoy! Hoy!* Hither! Flay him, does he slumber? Hither! Here! Now! *Hoy!*"

The bear half-slid, half-crawled backward. The air in the hole was thick. "Bring bracken," he said. "Bring all the bracken that be. Not all of ye!" he called sharply. "The crew of the first third—go!" What might have been confusion was at once averted. "The crew of the second third—to that line of tunnel where the pit props be fallen and bring, for the first fetch, the smallest and the softest pieces of the dry-rotted old props—"

He waited till they had got them gone and next he said, "Senior Aar. We must needs soon make fire."

A moment, then the elder nain murmured, "Ah, Bear, that be no easy thing, thee knows."

"I do know!"

"They take care—and always have—the accursed smoothskins, that we have no flint about us—to name but one lack—and though we might break the pick-handles, their wood be not—"

"And this, all this, I know. And *thee* knows and all of ye know what I mean. Well. The cub and I will withdraw."

Softly, as it might have been reluctantly, the senior nain said, "Nay the twain of ye may bide. 'Tis no time to stand upon custom."

He made a sign to the remaining nains and, though somewhat slowly, they joined hands. There was scarce room even at the broader end of the Doe-Hare's cave for a wide circle, shoulder to broad shoulder they stood, hand in hand, leg against leg and foot against foot. All was silent and, as silence will when thought upon, silence gradually gave voice. Silence whispered to itself, and silence began to sing a little song. It was a curious bit of song and it hissed and it crackled as the nain feet shuffled, as the nain forms shifted themselves in the darkness, as the small and cramped circle went around and around in the darkness, softly stamping feet upon the rubble-strewn floor.

Arnten stared into the blackness and, as it will when stared long into, the blackness began to give light, a faint blue light, a spark, a worm, a glow that had no outline and faded. And then did not fade.

Arnten felt the hairs on his flesh rise as his skin puckered in something the far side of fear. He saw in the darkness the forms of the nains and he saw their hairs risen and he saw upon that nimbus of hair outlining each head and each body a nimbus of blue light: and as the nains so softly-softly muttered the lights wavered and as the nains slowly circled around the blue lights slowly undulated and as the nains slowly and softly stamped their feet the blue lights softly hissed and softly crackled.

The dance did not cease when the first crew returned, arms laden with the great coarse bracken-fern; Arnten gestured and they passed their burdens, bundle by bundle, to the end of the cave. First they stuffed it through the still small opening into the outside world and then, when this would take no more, piled it all around about.

Then the second crew began to come back, stripped to the buff, their garment-skins used as carry-alls for piles of wood from the fallen pit-props, soft from long dry rot, and Arnten gestured again and they piled wood on the bracken. And still the slow, strange dance went on and on. Arn, in a few words, bade two more crews begone. They must bring back the larger stumps and shafts of the wooden columns used here and there to hold up the tunnel roof.

The dancing nains, meanwhile, had danced nearer and closer to what was now a bosky mass of dry-rotted wood and bracken. The dancing nains were pressed together almost as though to make one enormous grotesque creature with many limbs, a sort of nainipede; and this grotesque heaved and huddled close to the piled up bracken-fern which had been its bed. Still it sang and still the blue lights wavered at the ends of its hairs; and then the blue light gathered itself together into one mass and the nainipede went dancing back on its

many limbs. The ball of light floated up and
bounced along the rough roof of the cave and settled upon the pile of wood. It seemed next to snug-
gle and to creep its way deep into the bracken and
then there was a flash and the blue was gone and
there was the familiar red and orange and yellow of
fire. And the song was silent but in its place they
heard the crackling of flames.

Mered-delfin stood by the curtained door and
flapped wide black sleeves.

"My men have them safe now?" the Orfas demanded.

His chief witcherer opened his mouth and closed
it, long thin tongue fluttering. Then he said, "They
will not go."

Then seemed the king confused. "How now?
Won't go? The nains?"

Mered shook his dry old head, his long nose
seeming to point all ways at once. "Not the nains,
King Wolf! The men! Your men! The kingsmen
will not go! They will not go down into the mine!
It seems—I should have remembered that—" His
voice stuck, came out again at last. "They fear the
deep, they fear the darkness, assuredly they fear
the nains and their witchery."

The old wolf let waste no time in rage and im-
precation, but he rubbed one rusty wrist with one
rusty hand and he said in the voice of one who
thinks, "Then what is it which they may fear e'en
more, my crow, than the nains and the deep and
dark—eh?"

They looked at each other. The King's eyes went

111

past the old vizier and the old vizier turned; and together they exclaimed a word.

So dry was bracken and dry-rotted wood that both together burned with minimal smoke, but smoke even so there was. Arn and Arnten and the nains stood in the main corridor and with their garment-skins they flapped and fanned away the smoke. And now and then they stopped and took sips of water from the buckets, but only sips. A thin glow of firelight lit the somber halls of underground and over this lay a thin haze of smoke. The fire dance of the nainfolk had ceased.

He leaned against his father and in his body he was in the mine-cave and beside his father, yet in his mind he was beside his old uncle in the old man's medicine hut. And there was the sound of a dance . . . the sound of a drum . . .

Out of the dimness and the deep, deep darkness came the figures of men. It was no vision or dream—here, in the mine and out of the darkness of the mine-tunnels, they came.

"The guards," said Aar. "Aye, ehh'ng, be sure, be sure, 'twas that skulk-crow as sped the word to their crank lord." And in the nain-tongue he said a word. The men came not fast ahead, they moved slowly, irresolute. And in the dim glow of the fire and the thin haze of the smoke the nains began another sort of dance. They moved their feet up and down and they leaned forward and they waved their long, long arms. They did not actually move an ell along the tunnel floor, but in the misty, swimmy light, dim and flickering, it seemed as though they did move, did advance; and the men, moaning, dismayed, retreated.

Then at the edge of his ear Arnten heard the sound which had tapped below the surface, the thin *tap-tap*, *tump-tump*, of a witchery drum. And the soldiers milled about, cried out in alarm and unease. A spurt of fresh air cleared vision for a moment and a way ahead and now it was Arnten who cried out and a murmur went up. For back, far back, as far back as they could see in the main corridor came a marching column, a marching double column, a dancing double column, of figures which were manlike but were no men, a-waving in their tiny hands the menace of tiny spears.

And the witch-drum beat and the witch-things came and the men cried out and turned and turned.

Said one nain voice, amused and scorning, "Do they come at us with mandrakes, then? Nay'ng! The children o' the forge know a power or two for that."

Swiftly said the elder Aar, " 'Tis not against us that they deploy the mandrakes, 'tis to force on the men o'the king, who know no power, let alone two, for that."

Arn, without one word, picked up one of the water buckets and went straightway into the smoke-filled hole of the hare, pausing a moment at the entrance to pick up a fallen bit of bracken and dip it in the water and crush the dripping frond against his nose and mouth. In a moment came a hissing sound and a cloud of steam rolled out and all firelight was quenched.

But not for long, for torches now made appearances farther down the main corridor. The men, fearing the mandrakes more than the nains, came closer.

Arn emerged, stumbling, seized another bucket and again entered the cave. Again there was a hissing and a sizzling and again a cloud of steam. And a long pause—and Arnten held his breath and feared. And then the bear emerged again.

"The fire be out," he said, low and urgent. "And now it comes time to take these two last buckets of water and toss them on the hot rock. Do they crack well, we may all yet take our leave. And if not—" He shrugged. A huge mass of smoldering bracken was dragged out, picked up, heaved toward the advancing soldiery—who cried out, fell back into the smoke and gloom. And the drums beat and the mandrakes moved.

Now, all at once, all were in the place whence the hare had fled. Somehow there was light, light of a thin gray sort, obscured by steam, by smoke, but light. And Arnten felt the floor hot, hot against his feet and hissed his pain. He saw his father toss one bucket, heard him toss the second. Heard a cracking sound. And a second. Heard the nains give cry to their satisfaction. Heard the almost desperate cries of the kingsmen as they charged. Heard the sound of spears striking against wall and floor. Heard the sound of spear striking against flesh. Heard his voice raised in a wail as he saw his father stumble upon one knee with one spear into him. Saw Aar-heved-heved-aar fall and saw him crawl and saw him writhe and heard his death rattle.

Saw Bear seizing the very rims of the hole of the rock and smelled his flesh burn and saw his shoulders writhe and saw the rock face crack still more.

114

Cried out and wailed again as he saw his father turn toward him, face grim and hideous and smudged with ash and soot and blood spurting from nose and mouth. Saw that protruding from his father's flesh which he knew was the bloodied head of a spear. Felt his father seize him up and swing him around and protect his smaller body and thrust him through the hole in the rock whence came the milky light of dawn. Felt the last great thrust of that great body and saw the mine vanish from sight and felt the hot rock graze his side and saw the sky and felt himself fall. And roll. And move, crawling, crawling. Leaves in his mouth, dust in his nostrils, smoke all about him. Then no smoke about him. Writhing on his belly like a wounded snake. No more smoke. Shouts and cries in his mind alone. Then silence falling in his mind.

His father.

His father's face.

His father's deed.

At this last moment his father had said no word. His deed had been enough.

Chapter IX

The outlands seemed somehow not the same as before, but he had not the time to let his mind consider how or why. It had to concentrate on three things and the first and greatest of these was to make good his escape. For the moment he did indeed seem to be free—at least he could hear no sound of pursuit, and, now he had paused, could see none either. He had hidden himself in a thicket to do his necessity. Partly, this was automatic, for the commonmost ingredient of maleficent witchery was anything which had come from the body: what one could not burn, one buried; therefore all such doings as combing the hair or cutting the nails or easing oneself were done alone and unseen. And, his being in the bush was further pragmatic, it would enable him to see others before they could see him. His eyes peered about through the leafy screening, but the only sounds he could hear were birdsounds and the only moving thing he saw was a crow flapping its way above. *Nine generations lives the crow* was an old wiseword. Nine. Nine . . . What else was nine . . . a babe was nine, no, ten moons . . . but . . . ah! *Nine days lasts the shuddering bear.* Yes. He had not asked Arntat about that, and now— He pressed his cheeks up tightly and saw the thicket melt into his tears. Well, perhaps he had made good his escape, that was one thing. The second was that this alone was not enough, that he had to make his way to wizardland and feed the wizards there. And the third was, of course, that he could hardly think of actually making his way thither anymore than he could think of swimming across the all-circling sea to the barbar-lands. Where he and his father were for reasons unfathomable supposed to have been, he thought. And he thought about those far-off places, and of the land which had no end. Someday he would go there. As for now— He had in his hands leaves picked up to clean himself, and as he moved now to do so, he looked at them without knowing why, this time not carelessly but carefully. And realized why the outlands now seemed not the same as before. It was no longer the season of the spring and of the rich, swift-rushing green of everything. It was through the summer that they had toiled where no thing grew. And now it was the early fall, the last moments of the ripening: and then began the wither and decay: and then the long, slow death-time which was winter.

And when that time did come, where would he be?

When next he climbed, first a hill and then the tallest tree upon it, he did see men, near enough to make no doubt of it, and some had the white headband of couriers and some had not; he saw a wedge of swans flying south and heard their magic trumpet-call, high up. "Tell the nains I live!" he cried. "I live, I live! And have not forgotten!" and the wedge widened and then narrowed as it was before and the wild cry answered him. He saw beneath him a crow again, which might have been the same slow-flapping crow and—perhaps the hills threw back sound from side to side, warping as the water warps the image of that beneath it—its caw and cry sounded more like a man mocking it than a true corby itself. Arnten gripped the tree and hunched and peered at the distant figures, smaller than mennikins, mandrakes ... man-ant small. Like ants now they began to swarm, the croaking of the crow grew fainter and ceased, the men defiled westward, towards the sun's own line of descent, the bits of white bobbing. Then all were gone. Arnten relaxed his grip upon the tree. The sun slanted down the sky away from him, the kingmen sloped their arms and legs away from him. He was at least safe for now, he could not know if they had found a false trail, if they were hunting a trail true but another's, if they had abandoned pursuit—

For now, at least, he was safe, and that was enough.

He had fled too fast to find much food, but though he was hungry and gaunted, whatever he had eaten however long ago he had eaten it, it was enough. He had fled too fast to take much rest, but whatever rest he had taken however long ago he had taken it, it was enough. And all at once, now he was safe, it ceased to be enough: his empty gut gnawed at him, and weariness hit him like a club.

Tightly, he gripped both branch and bole, fearful of falling, then forced himself to loose his grip and—slowly, slowly—to dismount the tree. He came down more warily, as more wearily, than he had gone up: slip, pause, heart beating fast, a groping and a gripping with his farther foot, nigh one half-doubled against body, and cramped: something cracked—slipped: frantic grappling—lunge: all safe, for now.

But one hand was wet with sap where . . .

He pressed his face to his gummy hand, licked at it without looking or thinking. It was sweet, but it was not (his sudden thought) maple-sweet. Recognition and fear came together: honey, bees, swarmsting. He wanted at once to be gone; he at once wanted to eat his hunger-belly full of honey; he wanted to keep from any sudden motions which would alert the bee-guards. And as he clung, motionless as he could manage, one eye only with its unbidden roving told him anything, the other being too close to the tree itself; and this free eye told him that the nest was as full of comb as it was empty of colonists. He got another grip, crept around for a closer and further look. He held his breath and hearkened. There was not even a breeze to rustle the dying leaves. Perhaps he heard the faint, coarse clamor of the Corby-crow; perhaps it was in his memory alone.

But of humming or of buzzing, the dead air brought no hint.

He hesitated no longer, though he wondered much: thrust in his nearest hand, filled his mouth with wax-comb, honey, grubs, and all. And chewed and gobbled and swallowed and sucked. For long moments his mind and face were blank as a babe's while it nurses. Then the thought welled, like water bubbling up through sand, *I will take some to the nain-friends and to my father-bear*, and then over the dampness and sweetness of the honeycomb in the hollow of the tree came the dry and sour stink of the ore-caves and the smoke of the burning bracken. And the rush of memory burning like the bracken fire. How many of the nain-friends could still live? Few or none. And Arntat, his father, close mate of his captivity, his comrade was beyond question dead, and he thought of how he died. And tears washed runnels in the dust of his face and, mingled with the sweetness of the honey, he tasted their bitterness.

The salt was yet on his tongue, and bitterness and hatred fresh in his heart, strength new in his limbs, when he prepared once more to descend the tree. And realized in one swift second the wrath and guile of the wolf-king still quick against him, for the kingsmen had this past while and past his sight been half-turning the circle, and now—from dead opposite where he had seen them last—all broke the cover of the forest to find and take him. He saw them. They saw him, too.

But they did not see him soon enough.

They were stronger than he and had fed better than he had. All their lives, in fact, they had fed better than he had all his. But he had now eaten more recently than they and the hour past while they had tramped and trudged and forded streams and beaten bushes, he had rested whilst he was eating. And, too, they ran for him as men run for a prize. But he ran for the greatest prize—he ran for his life. He thought, as he fled, how it seemed that he was either bound or fleeting, always. It was his weird to flee, to be caught and bound and so to flee again. So now, strength renewed, he fled the kingsmen. He fled to remain free, to avoid another closing of the circle. In his freedom lay his life: but in his life lay . . . what?

If he fed the wizards he would find the cure for iron. It was half in his mind that it might be better if iron died: would not then Orfas, who was king by virtue of his iron, die with it? But the nains said it would not be better, and the nains were his friends, had been his father's friends; now that his father was dead they were his only friends . . . unless old Bab-uncle did still live . . . And somehow it was never at all clear in his mind, but somehow he dimly understood that iron was a thing of such great power that he who could cure its present ill must share somehow in that power.

And, so sharing, must thereafter needs never flee more.

So the pictures formed and shifted in his mind, and all the while he thought upon them, still he fled. He fled knowing that he should head north, where Nainland lay—and beyond, incalculably beyond, Wizardland—but *north*, here and now, was a way full of broken hills and jagged rock, gorges and cliffs and footing uncertain by reason of land-slip and scree. It was fine country for evasion, if only it was a country which well he knew. But he did not. And to break leg or neck was by far too high a price to pay.

Vaguely, he thought he had seen a gleam of water from high up in the honey tree, between the north and the east. Water was an invariable, a commonplace necessity. The country roundabout did not so much lack for any springs and brooks, however. It was not drink alone he had in mind. It was no pool or pond he had in mind, filthy although he was from his long imprisonment and from his late journey of escape, and much though he would like to bathe. Did not the hunted deer whenever possible seek to lose his pursuers in river and in creek? And now, pausing a bit to press his ear to the mossy earth, and (as so long ago) noting no sound save the beating of his own heart—now he remembered what else a river meant to him.

It meant a reed, and a greenstone, and a beech-nut, and a bear's claw. It meant his quest for his father. It meant another hollow in another tree. It—

Something flashed in the corner of his eye, quivering and bright as a butterfly, full of colors as a rainbow. He turned, slowly, slowly, fearful of los-

121

ing full sight of it as he also drew himself from the ground. The perry stood on the moss as though he would leave no print when next he moved. The expression on the perry's narrow face was half-smile and half-dream. It was the perry-look he remembered from the twilight of the time when he lay healing in the dim green bower, after the Painted Man had half-killed him. A sight—and even now the memory of it made him hiss and glance about in terror—as frightful as that of the perry was joyful: and yet a joy full mixed with awe.

The perry beckoned to him ... Did it not? It must have. He approached, holding out his hands. The expression on the slender, golden face deepened. It ... beckoned ... did it? He came on, feeling his face moving, his own face, feeling it glowing under the glancing of those glowing eyes. He spoke to the perry, and the perry spoke to him. That is, the perry *did* speak to him ...

And such a game that now the perry played with him, now hiding, now flashing into sight, now spinning in a whirl of gorgeous color, now vanishing behind a tree.

And, gleeful, joyful—though his sense of awe in no way abated—Arnten himself went spinning round the tree. He went round and round the huge, canting, slanting beech tree. The perry was not in sight, and he danced between the lengthening shadows as he waited for the perry to show itself once more for the game to go on. Then he heard the river, then he saw its waters flash, then memory flashed inside him, he suddenly went backwards and down, landing without pain ... and, looking up, saw that other hollow in this other tree. Saw it was indeed the Bear's tree. Knew it was impossible by any way of thought or walk or run for him (for them) to have come this far in such time as it took his shadow to grow that much longer. Knew, nevertheless, that it was that very tree: was this very tree. Was here.

And knew at last, with mingled sense of joy, of home, of safety, loss, grief, bewilderment—a sudden rush of tears and a cry which came from his very heart and echoed in his ears and danced back and forth across the silence—he knew that behind no bush or shrub or anywhere more, was the perry any longer to be found.

And never would that fire whose dead black scar he recognized dim upon the ground ever by any blaze see Arntat, his father-the-bear, again. *My heritage to you is otherwise.* And what was that heritage come to? A handful of memories, a witchery-bundle, and a bearskin. And to this heritage had the perry brought him.

Arnten got up. His dark face, now darker than ever—as was his lengthening, broadening body, with dusky bloom of hair—twisted, grimaced. A sound started, deep in his chest, rose to his throat and broke there, without ever becoming words. Sorrow was in it, and rage. Defiance. And regret. But not acceptance. Never that. Something was growing, and he was growing with it. Something with many plies. The perry was in it, and the nains. The hatred of King Orfas in it, too. Bears and hares. Crows, too. Iron, dying. Bear, dead. Wizards famishing. Great horn, many blasts. Beckoning of so deep a sleep that—

Anger beckoning, calling, hot and red. A nut falls

123

and rots and splits its skin and something like a
worm or snail creeps slowly out, lifts its blind head.
Let dust and mold of fallen leaves and mud of
many rains cover it, still it will go up ... up ... He
had felt these things in mind and blood and flesh.
He leaned against the rough bole of the tree. No
father, no brother, no comrade. But—up—

He came down this time without hesitation or
fear or any trembling weakness. Red were the hills
and faraway. It was half-time between the sun's
lower edge touching the farthest hills and its upper
edge slipping behind them. The witchery-bag was
round his neck, the bearskin round his shoulders.
Its smell was strong, strong, powering strong. And
how soon and smooth and swift he was half inside
it. Then he stopped. Something halted him, something turned him. Half walking and half shuffling,
clutching bundle and loose hide, he made his way
through the thickets heedless of waning light, along
a trail he saw without seeing it. There was the hole
and he had to go into it. The same strong smell as
the bear hide. He was all inside the hole, all inside
the hide. The bear was in the blood and now the
boy was in the bearskin. The bear remembered the
boy, forgot the boy, turned, fell, caught the dark.

He caught the dark and held fast to it to keep
himself from falling. He fell, sick and dark and
dizzy, and the dark fell with him. He clutched the
dark, and, feeling it stir, he grappled with it. The
dark resisted, fought with him; for long he wres-
tled with it, now he floated, not knowing up from
down; now he felt himself flung about. He groaned,
cried out, wanted only to rest. But the dark was

stronger, wilier. Sick, sore, vertiginous, confused, he felt his holds loosen. The dark disdained to slay him after such an easy victory. The dark shook itself loose, and with slow dignity, departed.

The young bear heard his strong young heart slowly pounding and he saw the young sun slowly dancing to the slow rhythm of his heart. The sun was pale yellow, and pale yellow were the flowers of the field and forest, a hundred and a thousand of them. A hundred suns blossomed and danced in the field and a thousand suns bloomed and swung in slow sedate circles in the forest and the field, to the slow thump-thump of the unseen drum. The sun was pale orange, and pale orange were the leaves of the trees, and suns as countless as the forest leaves fluttered in the air and danced there, and the floor of the forest was heaped with the orange-russet of the orange-russet suns. The sun was blood-red and blood-red its bloody drops fell slowly, slowly to earth, dancing as they drifted, a-
dance and a-
drift and a-
drip-drip-drop—
bloody leaves falling from the bloody trees great drops of dark blood bleeding from the bloody heart dancing in the aureole of bloody mist in the center of the sky, shedding its falling drops to feed the thirsty forest and the parching fields.

To warm the chill earth with its heavenly blanket.

The young bear stretched its supple limbs and felt them slide glide so smooth beneath his skin and each movement was a move of joy. He snuggled beneath the blanket and he slowly slowly turned about beneath the blood-warm leaves so warm so full of joy. The sun-heart long beating and bleeding slowly in the slow joy sky and the rings of bloody mist swung around and around, and the hearth-sun sang as it burned in the center of the sky. Red-hot embers drifted down from it to warm the chilly morrowing of the rime-white fields, and they hissed a singing as they sank so slowly joyly through the rose-red sky color of salmon-blood-flesh color of clear red honey blood joy fire circling dancing in the higher fire . . .

Every ember was a bear and a thousand hundred bears slid slowly turning dancing singing from the center of the sky and hummed upon the earth, sinking sliding gliding beneath the blanket of the earth ever deeper deeper into the ground, whilst the sky grew smaller smaller joyful smaller turning turning bright blood disk singing turning circling swinging singing so far far far from the blood warm center of the warm warm earth. And the russet circling small sky drifted higher and farther away, the orange sky as the bear stretched all its supple limbs in joyful extension, as the yellow sky small as sun was far away and pale pale pale, was white was cold was white white white was a turning dwindling point of white a dwindling turning speck of light

The vanished world outside was cold and gone forever from the blood-warm slower beating slower beating drum heart drum head drum hide slow beat slow beat slow

slow

slow

The forest was old, with hoary thick naps of moss upon the massive limbs of even its younger trees. The forest was old and had all but covered every trace of the last great fire to scar it, of the last great snow to break its boughs and the last great freeze to burst apart its limbs and even heart-wood. Increasingly now, as the slow wheel of the seasons turned its way through autumn, the true forms of the trees were revealed in their nakedness. The mantle of leaves had dwindled, was going fast, was almost gone. When clad in rich green robery, the forest might have passed for young. But that was over and gone now, and the sturdy age of every tree was increasingly to be seen: gnarled limbs still hearty, huge boughs stooping low.

The forest did not prepare for winter as the beasts do. Whereas each animal grew a thicker coat to shield and warm against the snows and blasty winds, each tree released its coat of leaves. Creatures of red blood shrank away from coming cold. But creatures of green blood let themselves be stripped bare, and if here and there clusters of leaves yet clung to limb and bough, limb and bough would shake them off before long. Massive and twisted and aged, the trees began to face the stern sere skies of winter, and with stern joy to bear the frigid mantle of the snows.

But now the air but tingled, and frost-nipped fruits ate well from bough or ground, and sometimes the stripling bear shambled along and ate them sweet and tart where they lay among the molding leaves, and sometimes he rose upon his feet and raked them off the branch which still they clung to. Some had been gnawed by mice and the mice grew plump upon the sweet flesh of nuts which they found in whatever corners and holes they had rolled and hidden, and the bear ate the plump sweet mice. Beasts of horn and claw he encountered, and feared them not. Once or twice he smelled the rough, stale odor which was man, and calmly turned aside. It was the odor of living men, but also there was something of dying and decay in it. And he knew without reflection that this last was iron.

All time moved smoothly, and all space: there was peace upon everything and everything was right. He saw a great roan mammont which he had seen before, and for a moment, unaccountably, he felt strangeness and un-peace: the mammont blew softly towards him from his supple snout a greeting and respect. Once more, then, peace, and rightness.

But, as some creature may step his foot into a snare and ken it not, walking pace after pace and feeling not the loop, till at last he has walked the full length of the noose-cord and then feels a tug upon his paw against which he tugs in turn: as the bent tree, suddenly released, springs up and away, and the creature who had a moment before walked sure and certain is now flung aloft and then drops and then is brought up short with a jerk and then dangles, helpless, in pain, confusion, and in shock—

So the stripling bear which had been calm and had ease as stripling bear, as manling bear, as bear youngman (the bear being in the blood and the blood being in the boy and the boy inside the bearskin) saw the mammont, peaced the mammont, passed the mammont, and then was by the memory of the mammont moving mountain serpent snout spear teeth blood fear terror flight blood blood blood, brought up as short and as sudden and as shocked as though caught and flung aloft by a snare: was a stripling: was a bear: was a young bear: was a young man: was a young man inside a bearskin.

A sound bubbled in his throat. The bearskin was rank. How hard it was to breathe. Where was the mammont? How hot it was. And wet. And wet. His legs and loins were hot and wet. Far away was the mammont, far far off and almost gone from sight. It would not turn now even if *boy*, which it did hate, came clear out of *bear*, which it did not hate.

Boy came clear out.

There was a pool of some small size which lay upon the lip of the forest by the commencement of the plain. It was brown from endless years of mouldered leaves, but it was a clear brown. A stranger looked out of it, barely faintly familiar. The small, downy, dark child of endless years ago had gone, gone almost quite away, though a residue of memory as faint but definite as the residue of leaves in the pool still remained, tincturing the memory as the water was tinctured, with an ineradicable stain of terror: present, but not strong. In place of that swarthy chickling of a child was a young man, broad of chest and shoulder, long of limb, with a long gaze as well, and steady enough of eye. That eye had seen much, and much weight had those shoulders borne—the yoke of thralldom and the freedom of the bearskin alike.

The cool brown water enfolded him like an embrace and tiny bubbles formed along each hair upon his skin, hair swirling up as flesh went down and down into the clear dark pond, and hair floating one last moment on the surface, dark hair, before head bobbed over and went down, down, down to rest between the knees: bubbles breaking, then no bubbles, nothing breaking the surface, surface gradually becoming calm— Arms flung wide, heels and soles pushing against the bottom, knees flexing, face turned up and lips drawn back, the whole body leaping up and clear of the pool's surface as an otter leaps, or a fish, or a seal—and a shout, loud, clear, defiant and whole, shaking more leaves from the trees which stand and lean over the pool, benign and strong and patient. With a tremendous splash the naked body descends again into the pool, water pouring again over its leafy brim, and then scrambles out, hairs slicked flat against the muscled chest and back and limbs. Runs, hulloaing, round and round about the pool. Leaps up and knocks more leaves down. Leaps over long-fallen, mossy-thick logs, legs thrust out, man-parts dangling and bobbing. Shouts and stamps.

Comes to a halt and looks down again into the pool into the face of his water-brother. And laughs and laughs. And they laugh, pointing at each other. And the forest—each moment becoming less *forest* and more *trees*—the forest's trees laugh back at both of them. And the laughter runs and leaps from side to side, and the leaves fall and, falling, dance; and it may be that the leaves laugh, too. A swirl of leaves is seen laughing midway far to one

side, it is a perry, and then the perry is gone away
and the leaves drift slowly to the leaf-strewn floor.

The man wraps his bearskin and walks naked
beneath the naked trees.

Chapter X

In a place favored by moonlight, where the mandrakes unfold and lift their faces from their hoods
to drink in the silver light, an old man sat drumming a light and hollow sound. More than one
rhythm did he try before he found one to their
true liking: and he sat and tummed upon the
drumlet in his lap and watched them swaying forth
and back. There are indeed profuse accounts of
how to pull them safely from their beds, but no
mandrake entire can be procured this way, account
or not. First the seeker must find the key which
can alone control them, this key being in sound and
not in substance: it will do for any group of them,
for each one of every group of them has spored
from the same damdrake—it is not widely known
that if kept alive unto a seventh season and ex-
posed to dew and moonlight, they will change sex
and then spore—hence, the tune that one will dance
to is the tune that all will dance to.

Arnten, slumbering in the woods, dreamed a
dream of his past youth, and, awakening, found
that part of the dream persisted. He rubbed eyes
and scalp, then—this element of the dream not vanishing—he got up and went in search of it. Before

131

long he was able to identify it as a soft and hollow drum-drum beat, and, more particularly as a mandrake drumset. And there was a vision and a picture in his head of an old and heavy damdrake, ponderous and fertile, being slowly, slowly drummed along through the moonlight, not so much dancing as waddling. Till at length a proper place was found, and so saw the dam, with a sound not unlike that of a sow in oestrus, sink heavily and gratefully into the loam: then silence until a certain moment when she burst open and all her spores one slow second glistered in the moonlight: and then settled all round about the husk to filter down deep enough to ponder and to grow.

Arnten saw the drummer bent upon his tune, and he sat upon his haunches and waited and watched. By and by the drumming slowed and the waving of the mandrakes slowed, too. Finally they sank their heads into their hoods and then their arms fell to their sides and dabbled in the dust and in another moment the tiny hands were settled again in the earth and all was still. The echo of the drumset played in Arnten's ears a while and he heard the drummer sigh. Next he heard him say, "My sister's daughter's son, will you not come up and sit beside me here? I am loath to move just yet."

Arnten came and sat beside him. "Surely, then, uncle, I made no sound," he said, "neither did I cast a shadow, being in the dark as I was. And the wind is towards me. How did you know?"

"Nevertheless. You were near the moonlight and the moonlight drank of your presence, so to speak. And I felt your pattern upon my skin. It seems that you have grown much and are much changed in other things, but most of all I perceive that you are strong and well . . . See now these mandrakes: by and by, by moonpull and by music I shall draw them up without touching them, they shall of their own selves draw up their geminated roots and dance upon them. At first a little. Then back into the ground. Then later, more and more, and of-tener. At a proper time, they will leave the ground forever and follow me home—"

"A-dancing."

"A-dancing. None way other."

The old man looked at him in the silverlight, and said, "You are grown greater, and there is more to the *more* of you than size and flesh alone. It is my thought that you have found your father."

"Found my father. Found my witchery-bundle. Found my bearskin. Found even this here, under my arm: tis within this case, a thing called fey horn—"

The old witcherer said, softly, "Ah. All-Caller. So."

He said, softly, "Your father?"

"—Among his gifts to me . . . Eh? I found him, yes. And the kingsmen found us both. Set us to rip red iron-stone with the nain-thralls in the mine." (Stink, and toil) "Thought to keep ahead of dying iron. Vain thought. Twas mined and forged only to rust and rot. And so we all did rust and rot there." (Smoke of their burning bracken-beds, flare of guard-torches, terror, confusion, purpose stronger than death) "They be dead, now, nain-thralls and father. And, not for them, I'd be dead, too." He paused, his face and his throat moving. "There was room for but one at a time through the scape-hole

133

whence the hare had come. They pushed me through, first one. Then there was no more time, not for them, any. Never.

"And what say thee next, aye? 'Their death-word to me?' Aye. Twas of the wizards that they spoke. *Feed the wizards.* Aye . . ."

For all the Land of Thule had been fed with fear since iron had begun to rust and die, since the king had fallen sick, perhaps sick with fear; since his fear that foreign invasion would find him weaponless, since the exactions of his men had become entirely instead of merely intermittently remorseless. Since the forges of Nainland had grown cold.

Old Bab-uncle and young Arn talked long there in the silverlight. Through the silverlight and the shadows they talked and walked. Then walked without talking. Crawled a way, beneath ground. And once again were in the medicine hut.

For a long moment Arnten stood there, familiarity now so very strange, ears supping up the old familiar sounds, nose snuffing up the old familiar smells and scents, and—gradually, as they cast off the scales of darkness—eyes tracing the old familiar outlines. There on the low bed in the corner, something groaned and moved. All seemed as before.

"The old woman is not better, then?" he asked.

"The old woman is dead."

"Ah." No more to be said about that. She had not been entirely alive at any time he himself had known her. As to who, then, lay in her bed, moved and groaned, why, doubtless, the witch-uncle had found a woman, but not a young one—hence, one who groaned. But this neat construction vanished at once when the shadow-form on the bed sat up

134

with a start and demanded in a man's voice which Arnten knew he knew, "Bab, who is with you?"

"'Tis well," said witchery-uncle. He moved about the fire, and in a moment it blazed up.

Arnten gasped. "Tall Roke! I thought ... I saw you dead."

Roke gave forth a wry sound, half chuckle, half bitter groan. "And not you alone," he said. "I *was* dead. And therefore to be left for the carrion-feeders ... even though my breath came back to me, by and by, and I spoke to those who'd come to see how I looked, dead. Spoke? Cried, shrieked, babbled, begged—"

"'Tis past," said uncle.

"Never past, for me! My breath wandered in the Dreaming World, I tell you, half-bear. I saw the breaths of the other deads—they came not to me, though, but with their hands they motioned me away; and with their voices, like the keening of strange birds, tis this which they said to me: 'Back! Back! Go back, Roke! It be not your weird to be here now. Go back, and back,' they told to me." His hair, though it had been hacked unskillfully with a sharpened shell, was yet longer than Arnten ever had seen it; long and yellow it hung about his scarred face, and he brushed at it awkwardly with an arm and hand which seemed to move not quite right, but which moved.

"Wife and child have I no more, nor house nor friends nor other things which were mine. The dead lose all right to such, as we all know; nor gain they any such by coming back to life again ..." His voice was low, deep into his body, and in his face

135

there was something which Arnten had not seen in any man's face before.

Arn felt chilled. And yet he did not look away, there in the medicine house which was more dark than light, smelling of mice and of mandrakes and of many half-dried plants, as Tall Roke, whom he had seen die, looked at him straight and deep.

"But in return for what I have lost, somewhat have I gained, bear's boy; it concerns you, and as I look at you I see that much which is heavy has befallen you in the enacting of your own weird since last bloody day we saw each other."

And he lay back down, but beckoned the other two near to him: and long they talked together, and sundry things they showed each other, while the small fire was fed small sticks, and the smokes moved slowly round and round: and sometimes the smokes found their way out, and sometimes they did not.

Light were the early winter snows, but heavy the mood of the hamlet. The common and customary tasks of making ready for the time of cold were gone through—house-walls and roofs put in order, skins of fur cut out and sinew-threads prepared to sew all with for garments, meat and fish smoked and stacked and stored, and wood piles grew—yet the usual satisfaction of doing usual tasks was absent. Hunting and fishing with bone and stone and horn did not yield the yield of iron, and iron continued ill. Now the common central-fire was no longer enough, each house must fire its hearth and for each hearth-fire tax must be paid. The days of felling trees with stone-hacks were not to return as yet, and as each house sought the windfallen wood, it was necessary to go farther and farther away for supply. Taxes had increased and were oppressive, and were brutally collected. There were said to be spies. There was certainly uncertainty and fear.

Now and then voices of loud good cheer rang out, and usually they broke off as faces turned with lowering looks to see who was so ill-tempered as to feel well. Mutters and whispers were common by far. But voices all fell silent when in sight of the low hut in which all knew a dead man lived; and a man so suddenly grown in repute as witcherer for having brought the dead one to life again; and one who was known to be that Son of the Bear who had been driven forth to die only that spring, and who not only had not died but had grown out of all reasonable expectation and past all natural rate of growth. These things were ill thought of, but even less to be thought of was to speak ill of them aloud—if at all. And so to these three, wood and winter peltry—clothes and food—were by stealth supplied, though not, of course, supplied by all, and, of course, never out of benevolence . . .

And day by day the dread sight was seen of Dead Roke, as he leaned upon the other two, walking up and down, for all the world as though he were alive: and day by day the strength of his gait and the span of his walk increased. Whey-face and his speckled clan were much given to ill looks and long faces over this, shrugs of incredulity and sighs of despair, groans of horror. Gestures threatening the witchery three. None gainsaid them, but, in truth, being generally believed to be among the king's eyes and ears, they were much more feared and hated than they were supported.

One day as the three of ill-omen paced slowly back and forth in the lane, a fourth person came into sight ... stopped still as they walked away again ... approached closer to where they had been ... and so until, at last, they faced each other. Arnten knit his heavy brows, sore memories of boys beating one boy rolling in his mind. Then his memory focused and his face cleared. "Corm," he said.

The day was cold, but Corm's pallor was not from that, and indeed sweat was on his face. Crows congregated and clamored in a crook tree by the lane, and when they paused the three could hear his troubled breath. He said, "I am afraid. Oh, how I am afraid..."

Arnten with one hand took the boy's hand. With his other hand he took Roke's hand and placed it under his own. The boy's hand trembled. Slowly, then, slowly, Arnten drew his own hand out. And so Corm's hand came to rest upon Roke's. After a long while the trembling ceased. Corm said, "Your hand is warm, and it is longer than mine, and it is the hand of a living man, and not of a dead one."

Roke said, "The pain of my body was so great as it lay, broken and bleeding, that I felt I couldn't stay in it, and my breath returned to the Dreaming World. Even when all the deads called out and cried out to me to return, I would not. Then I saw the bear, The Great Bear, The Dream Bear, with his stars all shining through him, and he came towards me as though he swam through water, although he did not move at all. Then he did move, and he reached forth his starry arm and touched my bosom with his starry hand, and he said to me in his great voice, 'Return.' So I did return, and I lay in my blood and others came and watched me but none helped me. Till at last came Bab, by whose kindness and whose witchery alone I truly returned to life."

He withdrew his hand and opened his upper garment. "And as to what befell me in the Dreaming World, in the Land of the Breaths, in deads' land, here is the sign."

On his bosom, as though drawn in blood but perfectly dry, red as red against the whiteness of his skin, as long and as broad as a full man's hand, was the likeness of a bear.

"Now," said Roke—after Corm, with a hiss and a sigh, had looked at the mark and touched it and then looked at the other three in awe, and looked at them, having drawn himself up, in silent expectation—"Now let us go inside, where there is less cold, and fewer eyes, and fewer ears." This they did, and Arnten told Corm of what he had experienced, he showed him the bear-token and the bear-skin and the witchery-bundle and the great horn which is All-Caller: and Corm spoke of the increasing oppression of the people, of their sufferings from the sickness of iron, from the heavy exactions of the king, from their fear of his eyes and of his spies, of hunger, cold, witchery, and weird. And Corm knelt and touched the bear-things and was made one of them.

That night the Bear came to Arnten in a dream. The Bear was there, but said nothing, and Arnten

139

saw many crows; he saw himself make a gesture and the crows flew off. All the crows but one flew off, and somehow Arnten killed the crow and cut off its head and cut out its tongue and buried the head. And when he awoke and when the others were awake he told his dream. And they talked of it, and they made their plans.

"Who knows how important this may be," said Bab-witcherer, "in carrying out what must be done, once Roke is all healed and capable of doing all things once again."

Arnten left the hut in midmorning, and Corm followed a good space behind. The leafless branches of the old crook tree were thick with crows, like so many black leaves. They cawed their cry to each other again and again, and the dull cold sky echoed with their harsh screams. Arnten made a dash towards the tree and flung out his hand, as though there were a stone in it. Instantly, and with great clamor, the flock took wing and wheeled away … all but one, which uttered what seemed a derisive cry to its fearful and departing fellows, now making tracks across the sky, then muttered some softer syllables to itself. And Corm placed a stone in a sling from where he stood, behind, and swung and cast and the crow fell dead from the tree.

With a grunt of satisfaction Arnten took up the dead bird and cut out its tongue with the knife from his father's witchery-bundle. It being ill-luck to bring any part of a crow into a hut with the blood still in it, Arnten sharpened a stick and thrust it into a slit cut in the spike of flesh, and propped it so that it would dry in the heat and smoke of a small fire built outside the hut. "That was well-aimed," he said to Corm, and added, "It was well-slung, too—" He accompanied his words with a gesture, and knocked over the stick: the tongue was jarred loose. "This was not well-aimed," he said, stooping to pick it and the stick up. They both laughed; somehow Arnten took hold of the tongue first: this being so, he held it to insert the stick once more, but the tiny sliver of flesh was hotter than he had thought, and burned his fingers. Again they both laughed, and he thrust the burned fingers into his mouth.

As he cooled them with his spittle he heard the voices of children, though unusually clear and delicate, and unlike the coarse tones which he associated with the voices of men-children. In another moment he heard one say, "The eggling of the Bear has cut out the corby's tongue!" And another said, "Night-colored one who flies in day, you will tell no more lies!" and one said "Nor truths as bad as lies, carrion-diet!"

Arnten looked up, half-astonished. "Who is that?" he asked.

"I see no one," said Corm.

Nor did Arnten, looking all around and fumbling with the stick: only two snowbirds. Even as he gazed at them, and all round the trodden snow of the lane, the birds took wing, and began to circle. And again he heard the beautifully clear children's voices; one saying, "But the hatchling of the Bear has acted too late, for the crow hath already told the wolf," and the other declaring, "Ill hath he done in telling so, though ill doth he ever do. When the wolf meets the Bear, beware!"

"Nay, Corm," said Arnsten, half confused, half

141

alarmed, "did you not just now hear children talking?"

Corm said, "I heard nothing but the chirping and chattering of those twain snowbirds—"

"When the wolf meets the Bear, beware!"

"Just now! Just now! Heard you not a child saying, *'When the wolf meets the Bear, beware'*?"

"Often have I heard those words, and more often of late than ever, Arnten," Corm said, looking pale again; "but—'just now?'—again, just now, I heard nothing but the chattering and the chirping of that pair snowbirds."

Now the skin-flap door of the hut was thrust aside, and the seamed face of Bab-uncle appeared. He asked what had happened, and was told, though the telling was confused—as were the tellers. Bab looked grave. "Where did you bury the crow-bird's head, then?" he asked. Both boys looked at him in sudden guilt, shock. "You have not buried the head? But ... you did cut the head off, as the dream directed? Not that either ..." He made a gesture, and at once set off to the crook crow-tree, and they with him. He made a single gesture more, seeing the splattered drops of blood upon the snow, and nought else.

"The dream has been in part fulfilled," he said. "Let that at least be an omen of good for us ..."

Orfas crouched huddled in his peltries upon his litter-bed in the Room of Secret Counsel, his queen silent and watchful at his side, when a strangely faltering step was heard approaching. It could be no stranger, else had the mandrakes on guard all shrieked beshrew, but—

142

Mered-delfin staggered in, straightened, sank heavily to his accustomed place. "What doth ail thee, Mered-witch?" the queen asked, swift. And even the Orfas-King, for once forgetful of his iron and of himself, stretched forth a hand as if to offer aid, muttered, "Mered, Mered, what is this—?"

The chief witcherer let drop the arm which, with its wide black sleeve, had shielded his face. His lord and lady again besought his words. He shook his head, he flapped his black-sleeved arm. Then he opened wide his mouth. But no words came out.

Only blood.

Chapter XI

Deeper drifted the snow, deeper the miseries of the people. Piece by piece the emissaries of the king took iron, took amber, furs, took stores of food. Those who were slow to pay had their fires trampled out, or were made sodden with the piddle of the tax-collectors. Sometimes those suspected of withholding, concealing—sometimes rightly, sometimes not—had hands or feet thrust into the flames or embers; were left with only their burns for warmth. The four who dwelt in old Bab's hut (Corm finding it, although scant and crowded, better than his family's house, they liking not and cursing much his new-found friendships) heard the steps of the kingsmen going by, and though sometimes the pace of these steps did seem to alter somewhat, though the voices of the enforcers of tribute tended to drop at such times, still, at no time did any thrust a hand to draw aside the door-skin—to venture inside. The old man paid his hearth-fire tax, and the kingsmen took care (if not content) to let matters rest at that.

Within the hut, and amongst the four, the present paced slowly, hanging the future. It was agreed that they must leave, and in general they were in accord that their passage must be for the north. It was not the winter and its snows which deterred their going; if the land were thus made harder of passing, less was the chance of pursuit, or even desire of pursuit. But as they depended much upon the presence of Roke, his skill and strength and vigorous manhood, so they could not leave till both strength and vigor were restored to him. The medicine and witchery of the Bab-wizard had helped keep Roke's breath within him when his bones were broke and his mind wandering, and this same wizardry and wisdom helped him as he mended. But Bab dared not force the pace, and none dared force the Bab.

As for Arnten, although the walls of the hut were not as close as those of the mine-cells, still, he took not much pleasure in them. *The Bear is in the blood* ...

Now, as he walked abroad, in woods or within the palisaded village, he heard, almost as the echo of his footsteps: Bear: *Bear*. Bear: *Bear*. Where? *There*! There: *Bear!* And the taunt of other seasons was gone. Awe there might be, or not. Perhaps respect, perhaps none. Sometimes, unsought: fear. Hatred? Also. By no means always. By no means. But ... scorn? Contempt? Nevermore. He was now

144

the weight, if not the height, of any full man; and solid all the way through. He did not walk quite as a man walked, toes down first or heels down first, but placing his sole down firmly and flatly. His eyes were fierce, and those few who met them and had scorned him as boy, as "bear's bastard," son of a mad mother and a father no one knew, found them by no means forgetful. Snow fell unheeded on his sleek head and shag breast and limbs. Mostly he wore but one sole garment, and this was the folded skin of a bear. And it was sometimes said, of nights, and when mouth was pressed close to ear, that on occasion he would unfold the bearskin and crawl inside of it and then indeed go on all four limbs, snout swaying from side to side: *beware!*

Bear! Bear! *Bear!*

But to no one did he say anything when he met them, him or her, though were it *her*, his gaze might change somewhat, be less unseeing, less aloof. But he said no word. And he said no word when, quite suddenly, and without any alarm, save that two great clouds of birds swung circling back and forth, and some cried *Wolf!* and some sang *Ware!* and—whilst he had turned and with steady step, stalked towards his hut—quite suddenly before he could reach it the streets were filled with kingsmen; and the multitude of them was like the swarming of lemmings: although lemmings do not carry spears, lemmings do not surround a man as they surrounded Arnten. They marched him, slowly, down the ways between the houses, houses in row after row, gaping and staring and low-murmuring people in row upon row. And in the great open place where the common-fire burned, huddled all in wolfskins, face all reddled as with the rust of dying iron, and in patches, angry, suffering, in pain, and half-mad . . . at *least* half . . .

This one bowed himself forward a half-bow, said, his voice not weak, though hollow, "Kinsman . . ."

A whisper went through the crowd, as a low wind goes through trees. And again the Orfas spoke: "Kinsman's son . . ." he said this time. Still Arnten said nothing. The frozen wind whipped round the arms and legs of his bearskin, and the king seemed to observe, to take note of this.

A third time he spoke. "Son of my half-brother's son"—again the murmur-whisper of the folk—Orfas drew back his meager lips and the folk hissed as he showed his teeth, whimpered as he rose a palm's breath on his litter, cried, howled, howled, "*Bear* . . ."

Arnten said, "Wolf."

Abrupt, sat the king down. Silence for a moment. Said the king: "Withdraw the curse on iron."

Arnten said nothing. He knew he could no more withdraw the curse on iron than he could fly, but none would believe him; he could in no way better his case by denying he had that power: therefore if they would not believe, then let them fear. He was again a captive? No words denying his own puissance would free him. Therefore no words such would he utter.

Said the king: "See you not how the people suffer from not having iron weaponry to seek their meat? Curse me, you kinsman, as your father cursed me, having sought the kingship, too, but no more curse *iron!*"

Arnten said nothing. He knew the king believed he held his father's might, knew the king believed his father had cursed iron to destroy the Orfas-King, to draw the teeth of the kingly wolf and leave him with rust alone when the barbar-folk, armed with weapons of iron in full good health, came sailing and came swarming across the all-circling sea. And Arnten knew that it is far better to be feared and hated without cause than to be scorned and condemned with or without cause. If Orfas was so far from full sharp of wits as to magnify, and publicly, one whom he might easily have slain—

"Name what reward you will, and here, publicly, I vow you shall have it: *But withdraw the curse on iron!*"

Thick a croak overhead and some distance so, Arnten heard a raven mutter, *"The man-wolf, the iron-man, the rust-sick: weak . . .",* and in that instant he understood, he saw, he felt the strength of his knowledge within him. He thought, "I shall repeat those words, and so confound him—"

He opened his mouth, but, "Do you put on your wolfskin and do I put on my bearskin, and let us then and thus contend: half brother of my father's father: *Is it wolf? or is it only dog?*" were the words he said. And marveled at them, hearing.

No moan, no whisper, no hiss, no motion, movement, sign, from any there. Such words might pass between king and one about to die because of king; but by no other one dared they be even heard. Across the space between them he heard the dry sounds the king's mouth made. After a space of time he saw the king's face move, twitch, saw the

147

king's hands clench upon his pelts. Saw a grimace cross the king's face and change into something which might have been a smile. King Orfas said, "Do you desire, then, to don your bearskin? So. So. So. Be it so."

His blood roared in his ears as he slipped into his bearskin. He heard the roaring of many waters and of many winds. He stood there, arms out as a bear's arms are out, saw, though little caring, the king's mouth moving as the king spoke to his captains. He shambled between the houses of the men, not bothering to observe their awe-struck faces, not deigning to so much as growl at the company of the spearmen who surrounded him. Since it must be so, when it must be so, he would receive the spears as though they were porcupine quills, he would slay his score before he fell.

The spearmen in front and at his side, who had been all the way stepping sidewise and scraping their feet after them, crabwise, now stopped, spears still pointing at him. He heard those behind likewise halt. He had scarcely followed as to where they were going. Now he knew. Here was an old, old and stooping tree, some ways outside the palisade; beneath its roots was a cavity in which and round which generations of children had hid and played: but he had never cared—after once or twice, perhaps once alone and once not—to go there as a boy—it was called "the Bear Cave," perhaps had even been one, once, before the founders of the village had graven the first furrow and, casting down a woman in it, had furrowed her as well; thus establishing the place as one of human habitation, of crops and all things fertile. It was called "the

Bear Cave," and no phrase containing the word bear was very pleasant to his ears when it came from the lips of other children.

The spearmen, the kingsmen, all the king's party, had circled this stoop old tree about and at a distance had begun to make campfires. Then up came the king, Orfas himself, carried in his litter-bed. They set it down. He said, "Bear." He said, "Some might say *bastard*, I say but *Bear*. You are indeed Bear? And son of the true Bear? So. Go. Go there. Into there. Down there. To the Bear cave. It is midwinter, it is the time of the bearsleep. Die, then, Bear, Bear's son, Curser of Iron. Die the Bear death. Sleep the Bear sleep. And as closely as the bearskin girds your body, so closely shall we gird and guard your hole, your grave, the pit from which you shall not emerge till the full winter-sleep be over: For do we but see your snout, Bear-kin, do we see so much as your shadow before the full measure of time be past: then we shall hunt you from your pit, Bear, take you from your skin, Bear; we shall even take from you your other skin, Bear: and we shall smoke it and shall smoke you in the fire, Bear, and then we shall see, the Curser of Iron, bastard son of bastard blood, betrayer, slowly die, slower than iron dies, down, down, hunt you down . . ."

The Orfas babbled and the Orfas raged and howled. One slow moment as the spearmen tensed, faces drawn, teeth fixed in lower lips, aslant their fearsome eyes begazed him, pale their faces though they so many and he but one; one slow moment only Arnten stood facing the black opening beneath the snowy ledge. He felt no anger, no rage,

149

nor lust; felt no despair. He felt only lassitude . . .
and . . . oh . . . it felt right. There he had to go.
Sooner or later all men had thereunto to go.

With slow step, paying no further mind to the
howling king or to the silent folk, thinking of nothing but the inevitable and hence the welcome dark,
he shambled forward, he entered into the open
grave, he descended down into the pit, and thus to
death.

*Darkness and deep time and deep darkness and
dark time* . . . Time knows not the darkness and the
darkness knows not time. Yet time passes and the
darkness, too. Pale yellow suns rolled round and
round, and faintly the taste of honey. Ghostly fish
leaped in silent streams. Darkness visible, shock
ebbing away. And rest. And rest, rest . . . rest . . .
warm in the darkness and the cold outside, the outside cold . . . *ssswww* . . . breath . . . *ssswww* . . .

Swans flying, long and melancholy their trumpet
sounds. Elk trample through the breast-high snow.
The hunting cry of the great white ounce, the leopard of the snow. Deep in their nests the snow-
white ermine lifted their heads. Somewhere in the
snow, the ptarmigan, couching in cold, white upon
white, lifted their wings and beat them as they rose
upon the snowy air, like a flurry of snowflakes.
Mered-delfin made signs to the Orfas-King. Pale as
snow, the queen sat upright, alert, silent. Somewhere a milk-white hare made faint tracks in the
soft white snow. "Yet another hour or so," muttered the wolf-king. He was loathe to show himself
as yet. It was not his hour of the day.

Soon enough his hour would be. The dead bear

would be dragged forth and flayed; flayed, the dead boy inside. Let all the people see, let all hope die forever within them that any rule in all of Thule was to be expected save from the House of the Wolf. And then let the long-waiting, long watching, long steadfast, suffering guardians be released from watch and ward. And let them ravage, ravish, break, burn, and bare away. Let all of Thule take heed, let not for a single day, henceforth, suffer any pretender to the vulpine throne.

Mered-delfin made signs to King Orfas. The queen, too, turned her head. "What sounds are these?" she asked. Mered-delfin made signs to his liege and lord the king. "Sounds?" groaned the king. "What . . . ?" He lifted his head. Watched. Hearkened. Many people were now coming. Who had summond them? Who had given orders— Mered-delfin made signs, lifted hands before mouth. "What? Horn? Calling? Who gave orders? Sounding . . . what horn? No order did I give, and no horn have I heard. Only—" He lifted a hand for silence which did not altogether come, his face was strained, intent. "—only this wind do I hear, and—"

Wind, if wind it was, sounding very strange indeed. He scowled his bewilderment, his concentration. There were many things in that wind, indeed, and many images gathered suddenly in his mind in swift confusion. He seemed to hear the trumpeting of swans, and the bugling of elk, the coughing bark of the snow-white ounce; he seemed to see the ermine lifting their heads like serpents, amid flurries of snowflakes which were simultaneously snowbirds— "Out!" he said, low-voiced, abrupt, more than merely urgent: "out—out—have them take me out of this— *Out!* What delay is this? *Out* and *out*, or—"

Oh, how many of the folk were now there, standing in the snow! How the kingsmen turned their heads this way and that, unsure if they should maintain their attention as it had been all this while, or if their spearheads should now at once face the multitude of the townsfolk: and meanwhile and at the same time, what winds were these, what sounds, what witcheries?

The litter-bed of King Orfas came swiftly from his tent-house, and the bearers bore down in one straight line for the very center of the encircling guards and watchfires. The guardsmen closed in without present word or order round the figure of their lord. And the people closed in close all around the guards. And so they all—king and king's household and king's guards and king's subjects—closed in from all sides round about that old crook tree: and while the litter-bed of the king was but a few paces away therefrom, the snow at the base of the tree seemed to boil up from between the roots and in one second more, so swiftly that no eye saw the several steps which must have preceded it, there stood there confronting the king, gaunt but huge and with eyes blazing red with rage and arms upraised and talons poised to rake and with teeth and tusk bared to tear—

"The Bear!" all voices cried aloud with one voice. "Not dead, not dead, but risen living from the bear-death, returned hither from the depths below and from the World of the Deads as ever does the true Bear. *"The Bear!"* rose one great cry from many throats. For the length of that first flurry in

152

which snow fell up instead of down and for the length of that one shout *"The Bear!"* all stood as though painted on a hide: King: kingsmen: folk: Bear.

And then the scene dissolved into a thousand fragments, and some were fleeing and some had fallen, as though some had gone down into the snow to make obeisance as one does before a king, and as though some of sudden terror and fright had fallen dead; and there was blood, red blood, upon the trodden white blanket of the snow: but as to whose blood it was, or how it had been shed or who had shed it or why: none paused to ask or seek.

Chapter XII

Sometimes the howling of wolves was heard, now nearer and now farther; sometimes the white elks lifted up their snowy heads and spoke to each other, drawing closer, but not fearfully, before any of the men could hear the other sounds. The white elk had been waiting for them in a wide bare place in the forest, a quarter-day's journey from the township, as the four of them fled: one bear-man, one dead-man, one witchery-man, and one for whom as yet no name had been devised, except the one already his—Corm.

"I had told the tallys in my tallybag," said Bab witch-uncle; "I counted the notches cut into other sticks by me. I watched the moon and the wheeling stars, and the angle of the sun's shadows day by day.

"But of course, not I alone did these things. Orfas had powerful witchery in his own tent-house. My calculating showed that a good several days yet remained before we could or should suspect to see thee stir—"

Whisper after whisper, snow sliding from tree limb, snow falling from elk-hoof and fetlock, snow blowing from one drift to another. "Thee might never have seen me stir at all," said Arnten, his mouth and face passing swiftly from wonder to grimness to gladness to wonder again; "had not Corm summoned me by All-Caller," and his eye and every eye went to the great fey horn, swinging in its cover-case of dull red leather against Corm's side.

Some tinge of that same color came to Corm's face. "It bade me do so," he said, almost faintly. "It spoke to me in clear tones by night and it murmured to me by day. But I feared . . . till that time just a while before the king and all his folk went rushing out, came a wind, a great wind rushing, and I heard the horn say *Sound me* and I heard the Bear say *Summon me* . . .

"It seemed to me, as I lifted it, heavy and fearful to my lips, as I held it, fearful and heavy at my lips, it seemed to me as my lips trembled and my hands faltered and my fingers fumbled in trying to turn the setting so that I should summon and sound well and call aright, it seemed to me as first my breath sooned in it when first I wound that great fey horn, oh! —that I did hear all manner of

154

creature of sea and air and land, and I struggled, lest I call them all—"

Roke rubbed one hand, which was still slow to full mending, and said, soft, "It is called by name, All-Caller."

"Surely thee called the wolf," said Bab, "else why rushed he there so soon? But,"—seeing that Corm looked abashed, the dark old man, sunk and huddled in his many furs, reached out a hand all gloved in mitt and patted the youngest of the four—"but no matter, that: In fact, twas well, to that: twas good indeed and well indeed that the wolf did see the triumph of the Bear. How so many folk fled so fast," the old witcherer said, all in mild wonder, nowise gloating. And the snow-whispers sounded as he paused.

Roke rumbled, "And of full surety thee did call the elk. Who did ever see elk so near to mendwelling? Who did ever see even two white elk together, nay, and there we saw four! And who has ever heard, when twas not story-telling time, that elk should kneel for men to mount?"

Arnten's rumble, containing agreement without words, was deeper than Roke's. Out of the dark depths of the bearsleep he had heard All-Caller, heard it as his father's voice: *Arnten! awake! Awake! The wolf and carrion-crow are at thee— awake! awake! Arise!* All the voices of the wild world sounding simultaneously in his ears behind his father's voice, he hearing the sky-trumpet of the swans, the cough of the snowy ounce, wild horses screaming, the fury of the mammont and the chirp and chatter of small bird and bark and bellow of sea-creature, morse and seal, which he had never heard before but knew, but knew—heard also, as though laying bare and in intended concealment, heard the hungry howl of a sick yet still-fierce wolf—

Heard no crow.

Swam up, in fury, through the snow, lashing out at those he had wearily bent before, before the time of and on the way to the bearsleep: they now in full terror before him. Some bleeding, torn. Some falling face-forward before him, spared. Some, shrieking, ran. Kingsmen and townsmen: some, shrieking, ran; some falling face forward very soon before him. He heard the shriek of a frightened hare, the whimper of a sore-sick wolf. Turned to find *wolf*, turned to slay *wolf*, saw three men neither fleeing nor falling face forward before him, reared up against them, teeth and claws bared: heard them cry, *"Bear! We be yours! Bear."* Saw and heard one of them give one last blast on one great horn—

Heard no crow.

Muttered, now, leaning forward against the snow-soft neck of the elk, "My father said, 'Crow ...'" He looked up, and saw a hawk swoop, saw it flurry, feint and pounce in the flurry of snow, saw it pause a moment and then, having missed, begin its ascent again. He whistled, and it paused and hung in the soft grey air. "Saw you any crow, swiftwings?" he called.

"Nay, no crow," the hawk shreck down to him. "All have gone, me think, to rob the granaries and skim the stinking midden-heaps of men. No skulk, black form defouls sky or land, O get of the Bear."

"Tis well, swiftwings." His deep rumble-voice

156

declined into his deep chest, the others looking at him, Roke and Corm in awe, Bab nodding as at the but expected. League after league they paced swiftly through the snow, the elk avoiding the deep-drifted places where even their nimble feet would flounder. "Tis well," he repeated. "No crow: no spy." They nodded, understanding now what the bird had said to him, and recollecting what he, Arnten, had told them of what he had realized of the spyings of the crow; all fitting into place with what Bab had told them of Mered-Delfin, Corby-Mered, who had the crow for his medicine-creature.

It was wolf weather, but they heard, they saw, no wolf. Only once were they sharply disturbed, in hastening at full pace towards their first destination, when, all slouching wearily against the necks of their elks towards the close of one day, Corm's head lolled and then snapped upright— At his cry they all were at once alert, and called out to him.

"Did no one see it? Did I alone see it? Did I dream?"

"Ask no more, but tell instead: what made thee cry out?"

He seemed slow, fearful, reluctant to speak of it. Then, "What said the hawk to thee, Bear? Said he indeed, *No crow*—?"

Arnten, bear-man, son of the Bear, considered. His face still had somewhat of the gauntness which had marked his arise from foodless bearsleep, though he had eaten—it had seemed—full enough to make up for it. Perhaps it was but a certain sharpness which now lay upon him. His voice had deepened. He said, slow, "His word was, '*Nay, no crow . . . No skulk, black form defouls sky or land*' was his word to me. And now your word to me, Corm-hornbearer?"

Corm answered his question with another. "Is there . . . has any heard . . . ever . . . could there be such a thing, for there be indeed white elk and white leopard, and ermine and . . . could there indeed be such a thing as a *white* crow?"

No one answered. But no one's head lolled more. Each head gazed about, keenly at each snowy branch, slantly at each white-tufted treetop. And now and often each head was raised to try and pierce the secrets of the dull, concealing sky.

Only when they had paused, when the elk had found the sheltered and snowless side of some great thrust of rock, and knelt; only then, all dismounted and baggage laden off, twiggy branches gathered for resting place and small fire made; only when all had eaten and drunk the melted snow whose stale taste they now barely noticed, and sighed and composed themselves for sleep: only then did Bab speak.

"This time tomorrow should see us at Nainland," he said. And he said, "I trust that we shall be safe there."

The forges of Nainland were cold.

Uur-tenokh-tenokh-guur was greatly aged. His pelt was grizzled; his eyes, deep-sunken, seemed more often to gaze through them than at them. And, what Bab for one found most shocking, the old nain slouched and swayed slightly back and forth before them, slouched so that the backs of

158

his knuckles rested on the ground. It was the openness of this stance which Bab found shocking, not the swaying, for many creatures swayed so at times. That nains did sometimes rest and sometimes even walk, slouching, so, knuckles on the ground, all men did know. In fact, from this and this alone came the evil nickname of *shamblenain* which was sometimes shouted in their direction with much mocking imitation by children ... when the nains had certainly gone of out both eyesight and earshot. But it was unknown that nains or any nain would willingly act this in the presence of men, for they were, it was thought, as sensitive on this as the Painted Men were about seen by other men with unpainted skin.

"The forges of Nainland are cold," murmured Uur-tenokh-tenokh-guur. "Some say, Forge cold iron, then—fools! Forge cold iron, then—fools! Men-fools, saying, Forge cold iron, then ... spies of Orfas, eyes and ears of wolf-king ...

"But you are safe here," said Uur-tenokh-tenokh-guur, in the moment when Arnten was certain that the old chief smith did not see them at all, nor clearly wit that they were there. "You are safe enough here," he said, clearly enough, looking at them full wittingly, though unsurprised. The sight of him, the nain-burr in his voice, the strong old smell of him, for a moment Arnten felt himself begin to sway, was born back in memory to his vile prisonment in the Wolf-king's mines, smelled the burning of the bracken-fern which had been their sole bed, heard his father roaring as he held off the guards, having dropped him, then Arnten only, through the long scraped-at scape hole to safety—

he, for at least one more minute or two still only Arnten, the Son of the Bear. He stilled himself. He was Arntenas-Arnten now: in the Old Tongue, in the witchery-language, Bear-Man-Son-of-the-Bear. Or, merely—*merely?*—he himself was now Arn. Bear.

"Bear dies, iron dies," muttered the aged smithy-Chief. "Iron dying, Wolf dying. Bear sleeps death-sleep, so must iron sleep. Bear comes to life, so must iron. One queen is every queen.

Lion, tiger, wolf and bear;
Bee and salmon, mole and hare,

they shift their shapes . . . Mayhap Nains be dying, too. Uur-tenokh-tenokh-guur is cold. The forges of Nainland are cold." He muttered something in the Old Language, in the Witchery Tongue. Old Bab murmured something back. "Could thee vision such a thing?" the old man of the nain-forges asked his silent guests, swaying, caring not, on his knuckles. "I had never dreamed to see it, nor thought it could be seen. Smoothskins! Know'st thee all what I tell thee?" He quite suddenly shambled forward, they stepped back and away, he raised his hands and spread his palms and gestured them to go out before him and he followed, they hearing the never-before-heard-by-them sound of a creature of the sort who walks on two limbs now padding along on four. A moment more and they stood on the threshold of his lair. It seemed as though something at that moment had pierced the sky, the cold sun perhaps, for the day grew sudden bright and before them they saw, spread out over all as far as they could see, the stone tables all blackened with fire which were the forges which had once supplied

160

all Thule with iron, whose fires and whose smokes were proverbial, the sounds of which were fabled. The forges of Nainland lay before them, where once was beaten out all the iron work of Thule.

"No fire," crooned Uur-tenokh-tenokh-guur. "No smoke, no hammering. No sough, no blast. The hearts of Nainland have ceased to beat. The forges of Nainland are cold, are cold.

"The forges of Nainland are cold . . ."

But still fires smoldered, as though too cast down to blaze, on the inner hearths; and the ancient seemed—perhaps only seemed—younger, healthier, quicker, sounder, keener, as they all of them crouched with him, with him and some several other nains. Arntenas-Arntén had told them what he could of their kinsmen toiling in the quickeningly futile labor of the mines of iron round about which Orfas King had built his prison walls. Nain-thralls . . . the word came not easy to their mouths, mostly they growled it low, in their throats and chests. And they growled, sighed, when he repeated to them some few parts of the songs the nain-thralls sang, as it had been translated to him, sang as they toiled, slow dirgelike chanting:

> *Once the nains were free as swans*
> *And the nains see them . . .*

"Or did they think it truly, not thinking me to be a fool, but being only fools themselves? 'Forge cold iron, then'? Why—were the smallest hammer in all Nainland to beat one stroke on the smallest forge, Orfas would hear it, Orfas would say in his wolfish

161

heart, 'They nains have tricked me!' Did he not threat me he would come here with all his company of spearsmen? Some say to fear he not, but I say: Fear all smoothskins, walk lightly through all their lands, but make no smallest move which might make them walk through Nainland.

"Bear! What now?"

"This I hoped to hear from thee, grand-uncle."

"Why? How? Why?"

"Some had said so."

"What else, some had said?"

Arntenas paused, mused. Then, "Feed the wizards," he said. A great sigh, a groaning, moaning, like some odd wind, and in the dim light the thick bodies of the nains swayed like a grove of great trees sway in the wind: not much, not much at all: put perceptibly. Uur-tenokh-tenokh-guur gazed at the fire, his face now seemed greedy, he grunted a word, fire was built higher. He spread his nostrils wide, as though grateful even for the scent of smoke. Someone among the nains had picked up a stone, and gave it a crack against the stone seats on which they all sat or crouched. And another. Another. It was not, then, a forge-stone, and no one needed fear that the spies called the king's ears would hear it; but it beat a slow forge-rhythm and as it beat and as the nains swayed in the shadow and the smoke, the aged chief of all their smiths beat his fists upon his knees, and, beating, spoke.

He told them that iron was a living thing which grew in the ground, which breathed and sweated, that fire opened the pores of iron and that water closed them. Every wood has its witch, and every metal, too, that sometimes one entered the other

... by breath, by mouth, by pores. That nains could see the pores opening in firey iron (though this they knew) as they could see them close when quenched in water; whilest men could see neither; just as nains could see a sundry multitude of patterns as iron lay gasping in the hot embrace of the fire, knew how to work it, taking note of these patterns and particles. The nain-sense of such things was part of nain-craft, of nain-lore. Of witchery.

True, admitted the old smith, nains could not indeed walk in the fire as could the salamander, though, true, he stated simply, nains could hold iron far, far hotter than ever men could do. The old, deep-sunk eye glowed redly, no more mere amber.

"Past the forests and the heaths which are past Nainland, lie the Paar Marshes, and past them are the Death Marshes, and past them are the Great Glens where the wizards have their deep caves: but seldom has any dared go that way, for the airs of the marshes and the airs of the caves are alike intermittently foul and often deadly. It is when lightning strikes these thick murk mists that dragons are engendered. And as to what use these dragons may be put, these are not the concern of either nains or perries or of men, and certainly not of the gross barbar-folk who come a prowling, at times a-prowling, o'er the all-circling sea ..." Uur-tenokh-tenokh-guur's voice had fallen into something not unlike the storyteller's chant, the taletellers' mode: Arntenas recalled things his uncle used to tell round the fire hearths as the snow-daemons howled and prowled, of were-whales and tree-tigers and the bewitchments of the Painted Men whose skin must not be seen, he shuddered, recalling his own single encounter with one such; the memory as well as the old nain's words bringing swift reflection on perries; but this swiftly went from him as he attended closely and heard one by one the other nains join in and their voices sink into deep chant of the divine and dying Bear, who descends into death each winter and arises from his grave whilst still the earth in which his grave was made lay still locked strong in death.

And then they had gone on to something else, he heard them intoning, *"By what three things is a king made? By strength, by magic, and by fortune."* Had he not heard this before? Twas nain-talk. No nearer to his destination did it bring him. But ... "By three things is a king unmade. By fortune, by witchery, by strength." He sighed. Less than a year ago he was a child, eating offals, glad for bones: now he sat by the hearthfire of the nains. Let him, then, listen, bide his time, hold up his head, hearken well. Yet his head drooped. Then it snapped up.

"First comes All-Caller, the great fey horn," the old nain held the syllables in his mouth as though reluctant to release them. "Next comes True Iron. True Iron casts out false. Next comes Fireborn, first-born Son of Fire. Fireborn hews false iron into pieces. All is known to the wizards, but the wizards are known to few or none. The nains know iron, more ever than men do know iron, much more do the nains know.

"But there be things which e'en the nains know not, e'en of iron: and these do the wizards know. And if their mouths be closed, there is that which

164

will make them open ... food will make them open."

In his narratings he brought them now safe past the Death Marshes and into Wizardland, and told how there was neither game nor fish in Wizardland, neither grew there any plant for food. So had the wizards learned to go one hundred years upon one single meal, yet they can go no longer. They cannot be said to live. But neither dare one call them dead. And at this Uur-tenokh-tenokh-gurr slowly swung his shag old body and moved his great head upon its stiff neck and looked full at Arntenas-Arnten. And the chanting died away. And only the old nain was heard.

"Who else, not in Wizardland—who else, not a wizard—has in sooth and in truth gone longer without taking food, taking drink, than any nain or simple man? If not a hundred years, then one-third of one hundred days, and several days more? The Bear. The Bear. In sooth and in truth. The Bear. One has heard that the wizards know the reason for the death of iron. One has heard this whispered in the snows and heard it in the winds, and one may have seen it also in the stars. It may not be so. Not all one hears is so. But it may be so. It may be worth the striving and the risk. To go into the Great Glens to seek the wizards is by no means to go to certain death, else none had returned by whose accounts we have reason and kenning to speak. Let he who has gone long without eating go and feed those who may have gone even longer by now without eating; and let him not go quite alone, and let him bring them a meal of liver and

165

fat and marrow spread on a clean piece of bark and sprinkled with clean sea-salt.

"And let him ask. Then let him ask. And then let him ask about the death of iron. And, ah, and, O! Let him hearken and listen well, so well." His voice sank, sank, sank. *"For the forges of Nainland are cold."*

Chapter XIII

As his company was now increased to five, himself included, Arn-Bear had thought that perhaps he might find five elk waiting when it came time to move on. It was wry, how each of the first four in turn made as if to offer his own place as elk-rider to the new companion, and how each in turn, after a longer look, gave up the notion. Something in the new one's look seemed clearly to say the offer was not needed, would be better not made.

It seemed to them that he was young, as well as such things might be estimated of nains. To say that he seemed strong is to say that he seemed a nain. His broad back was well-packed with store of the increasingly scant supply which Nainland had to offer, and yet Nainland had given of that supply to the other four as well. And in one vast hand he held a silex, the nain weapon of ancient-most legend, antedating even that bronze metal which had died of the green-sickness long and long ago: hewn of glittering quartz flint: knife, with his own hand as handle—axe, with his long enormous arm as axe-haft.

Uur-tenokh-tenokh-guur was as they first saw him, now as they last saw him: slightly swaying as he stood and leaned upon the backs of his hand-knuckles. And his eyes were but dull amber eyes in the light of the pale cold day. But other nains there were who spoke, though he was silent. "Have you ever seen a like to this, then, Bear?" asked one of these, holding up a piece of hide, cured well. Arn knit his shag brows, his face saying plainly that he kenned not the question.

Something which might have been the husk of a laugh—if nains laughed—rattled in the nain's chest. He brought the piece of well-cured hide closer. For a moment still frowning, Arn looked closely at it, though the frown had already begun to melt in the awareness that there was no nonsense here. And then it was as though the piece of hide spoke to him. Frown vanished in a look of enlightenment which was joy. He reached for the hide's other end.

"Surely this green mark which turns and turns like a snake is no snake, nor even eel," he said; "but surely—here, for here I see it be marked with a fish!—surely this be river?"

"It does be river," said the nain.

"And here there is a—oh, it is like a medicine-picture—a witchery-mark, yet not: hills. These be hills and the river winds down the hills . . ."

"The river does wind down the hills," the nain agreed.

Most of the pictures, marks, symbols, Arn grasped. A few had to be explained to him. He did not know the sign for wizard. "Though I should surely in time have scanned that out," he said, with dignity. Arn was often straight with dignity those days.

"Surely in time," the nain agreed.

"This is a pretty device, this ... map?—this map," he went on, and then his sense over-weighed even his dignity, and he said, "I wish that I had had one sooner," he said, slowly. Then, very quickly, "Had I, then might I have found my father sooner, and been more with him whenas we were free." Something burned in his throat: the smell of burning bracken, the smell of guard-torches. Something burned in his eyes, too.

The nain said, "The Bear were friend a-we," dropping into his common speech, as though somehow embracing and including and understanding. Then, as before: "We cannot be sure of all painted here. Perhaps if you find something wrong, or something not on here—"

"I will paint it so as we go."

No palisades marked the settlements of Nainland, only the deep-set nain-lairs and here and there dark-stained places where charcoal had been burned, and thin lines of smokes from the lairs. And here and there a nain returning, usually empty-handed, from a search for food, making deep tracks in the snow. And, by every settlement, by every group of lairs, the blackened stone tables which were the nain-forges.

And each such place seemed to echo with the lament of Uur-tenokh-tenokh-guur: *The forges of Nainland are cold.*

Arn noticed that his elk had stopped, and the

others as well. He wondered if it were time for food, or a fire, or— His mind had been far away. He looked around and saw the young nain at his side, and now, for the first time, this one spoke: "I have never been past here," he said.

Arn blinked, cleared his eyes. A different kind of landscape lay ahead of him, very flat, and thinly covered with a different kind of trees, strange and tall and twisted pines, with black needles free of snow. "This is the end of Nainland, then," he said, not asking.

His new companion gave the deep click which was the nain assent. "Here begins the Paar Marshes," he said.

"Mark where the sun now stands," Arn said, "and so straight on." For a while he strained to think what different sound there was, then it came to him that what was different was the absence of a sound he had grown used to during the earlier part of the journey. The snow did not whisper any longer. There lay none on the twisted tall pine trees, none shifted with the wind, there was no wind. And none fell whispering from the feet and fetlocks of the elk.

The nain watched him as he leaned far over, holding the elk about the neck, and grasped up a handful of snow; then did the same. "It seems wetter," Arn said. "Heavier . . ."

"Twill soon melt," said the nain. And soon melt it did, for every day the sun was somewhat longer with them and no fresh snow fell. The pines grew blacker and blacker and thicker and thicker upon the flat ground. They saw fewer living things, for no grass grows, snow or no snow, where the pine needles fall full thick. No deer pawed for browse, no tracks were seen, save only here and there the light ones of a bird. Mostly the pines were bare of limbs till far from the ground, but presently they came to one so bent and gnarled that it was fair easy for Arn to climb. He had grown uneasy at having no hills to look about from.

Still the land was flat and nothing new did he see, till turning to scan the last fourth of the landscape, he observed smoke, and a thick smoke, so that at first he thought the forest was afire, or the grass: then realized it could be neither at this season: and next he saw that it did not act, somehow, as smoke did. So he considered that it must be mist. And so considering, descended, very thoughtfully indeed. Tall Roke looked wistfully at him, still too stiff to be mounting trees. Arn said, "That way lie the Death Marshes."

Their faces grew grom at this. Then Corm said, "Well, we must pass what we do not want to, come whither we do." He let his fingers rest a moment lightly upon the case which carried All-Caller. Then he smiled, though it was a thin, pale smile.

Roke said, "Always I heard, 'A-well, a man dies once only,' and fool word I thought it then. But now I find it a great comfort, for having already died once . . ."

Bab rubbed his hands gently upon the elk he rode. "It is a time yet," he said, "before we are to meet the Death Marshes. And I do not think that the marshes will go from their place to meet us before time."

Arn mounted again. "I saw no crows," he said. And thought to himself that twould be fortunate

170

indeed if he saw nothing worse. The air grew warmer, flatter, staler, the snow thinner, and finally vanished after some miles of a thin, bubbly skim which lay upon the ground, neither snow nor frost nor ice. They eyed this with mistrust, fearful that its end meant mud, that mud meant marsh; but the ground still stayed hard and firm. The trees were now less tall but, as though to make up for that, were thicker, both on the ground and round about each twisty boll. And black as ever. Next it came about that they could see the mists without having to climb, and he who climbed next (twas Corm) returned to flat land paler than before and announced that there was now mist afar off to another side as well. And so, as though at its own pace, slowly the marshes came to meet them.

They still walked on firm ground, but this had shrunk so that it seemed a road; there were still trees to either side, but they were now canted at odd and painful angles and sunken in pools of dirty, sluggish mist, which now and then cleared away to reveal pools of sluggish, dirty water. The trees seemed to be drowning, struggling and writhing in anguish to keep above the filthy and murderous surface of the marsh.

And next it seemed that they could hear them drowning, a thick, panting, bubbling noise, from behind the squalid mists; a hissing and a squelching sound, and then other sorts of sounds, of which not all were describable and all were horrid. Then horror slid out of the mists. It seemed to slide towards them without actually moving, then it stepped out of the mists and, walking on its now visible feet swift and stiff-legged, it opened horrid jaws and hissed and rushed upon the nain, who was as was his custom walking first. He cast his flint at it and they heard the blow and saw the sleek grinning serpent-head yield a bit and bleed a bit and hiss more and show teeth, but still it came on swift and stiff-legged. The head came down and the nain leaped up—how beyond all speech the wonder of that leap—catching with each hand the horrid lip on the under-jaw on each side, and the horror which had come out of the mist began to make croaking noises quite dreadful and dismaying to hear, tossed its head and again, tried to shake off this which would become prey, tried to reach it with one great claw-foot, and slipped, and tried again, and brought the grom slant head down close to the ground and raked the nain with its talons. Arn seized the flint-quartz and struck where he saw two bones that moment outlined between head and back, and struck again and again and struck again, and felt the talons ripping at his own body, and saw the slant head and its rolling serpent-eye and stinking teeth, and slid and slid and struggled for balance and slipped, and then was down and the head of teeth dived at him and vanished, and then as though hands had been plucked from his ears, he heard everyone screaming, shouting, the earth quagged and trembled, and he slid into the marsh and caught a glimpse of the head again.

Everything stopped there. Everything stopped. Very slowly then he climbed out of the marsh. Something was thrashing about hugely and heavily and gouts of mud and blood and water fell all about. This was not well, so Arn walked away from it and he saw his uncle lying on one arm and

watching the thrashing and he, Arn, very respect-
fully and without urgency helped his uncle up and
they went on their way. The next thing they saw
was Roke and Corm and the nain all on their knees
and scrambling in the muddy road and in the pools
of blood and water for the great piece of flint, and
it most seemed that they might fight over it—and
this would not be well.

Arn said, "This is not well, Roke and Corm. The
flint is the nain's."

So Roke and Corm ceased grappling and grasp-
ing and the nain alone reached and took it and
grumbled and said, muttering, "It is filthy." Then
he slowly arose with it in his hand and looked
about him, hand poised to strike. He blinked. Everything was almost silent now. There was a splash.
After a long while, another splash. After a long
while, another splash. Slowly, they all gathered
round the nain and looked. Something rather like a
huge fish or eel or perhaps snake came slowly up
out of the water on one side and slowly fell into
the water on the other ... with a splash. It lay
there. Then it began to rise. Then the nain stepped
forward, and as though trained as a team, the other
four stepped beside him, step—step—step— But
there was nothing more for a long while. And after
a long while the mists parted and they saw the horror lying quite twisted and broken across the ridge
of dry land.

"Be get us gone," someone muttered. "Do it
have a mate . . ."

The Bab, in a voice which now for the first time
sounded old and tired, said, quite calmly, "At this
season of the year no such creature has a mate.

173

Still," he added, as though considering a rather nice point, "still, I see no why to linger."

But linger they did, and the nain gave over his flint to Roke and Roke proceeded to skin the dead beast, and to cut the skin into manageable pieces which they wrapped wet side inside and bound about with strips of the same. Then they went on. Gradually the road (as they had come to think of it) widened and the marshes retreated, with their drowning trees and strange bubbling and other sounds. It is true that not all of the party quite shared Bab's belief that the great swamp beast (Corm called it "dragon") had no current mate, and Roke muttered there might be others lurking, even if not related at all. They watched carefully and looked over their shoulders till long after the last mists had died away.

The country the other side of the Death Marshes had no particular name; it was very much like their own country in the south of Thule, save that it seemed to have no manfolk dwelling in it, and their companion said that there were no nains there, either. He had considerably abated the withdrawn manner which had seemed habitual to him at first: when you have all been slithering in the muck and trying to escape dragon's teeth and claws, there seems little reason not to be friends: and he at length informed them, with a hint of a shaggy smile, that his name was Eër-derred-derred-eër.

As for the elk, witchery-summoned to their aid or not, they had fled at first sight or sound or perhaps scent of the swamp-monster, and for true, no one

174

blamed them. It was heavier work walking and carrying their gear, scant though it was, but the increasing geniality of the weather made up for much. The long, cold hand of winter was relaxed from their throats, and they all felt easier. They had eaten their winter rations without much knowing how long it would be before they got more: it had been Eat or perish. And now game was seen again, and green shoots to chew on; and there were fish in the streams. One by one the streams flowed into larger streams, and one day, there before them was the river of the hide map.

There before them was clean water running deeper than they had long seen, and they looked at each other and they laughed to see how dirty they all were. Roke declared that mere washing in water was not enough, and he set to a-building of a hut for steam-baths, Corm helping him. Corm was certainly more at home with witchery than before, but a steam-bath was a familiar thing, and perhaps in acknowledging how much he had missed it he was admitting how much he had missed other familiar things. He too had left boyhood behind him, and a soft down had begun to creep along his cheeks.

While Roke muttered fussily as he put the ridged crown on the small hut and Corm gathered wood and stones to heat in the fire, Eër-derred-derred-eër, who had selected a spot in the water which came breast-high when he sat in it, sat in it and bobbed himself back and forth, going under each time, coming up bubbling and burbling and spouting like some strange sea creature. Arn looked and laughed, cast his clothes at the brim, walked in

175

until he felt the waves tickling his ribs, and then gave a whoop and dived forward. He swam and floated and dived and whooped and did some spouting of his own, and it was as he gave a spectacular spout and turned over on his side that he saw the woman in the pool.

He felt the sun warm upon his skin and he observed her standing in the shadow of the birch trees; a faint calm smile she wore, and her naked flesh shone silvery in the dappled light. It was the easiest thing to swim over to her and to stand beside her under the shade of the birches, dappled with the same light, and to smile on her. Suddenly there was a flash and before he could so much as blink, she had gone, but he saw her under the water, her figure oddly distorted but still gleaming and flashing; and he dived after her.

Long, long they dallied and played in that river, chasing and pursuing one the other, and she showed no fright as he first touched her. He felt so many things. She was new, and had seemed so rightly to have become a new companion. She was so fair and beautiful, and he hungered after beauty more than he ever knew or would ever know till long later. And there was more, so much more that he felt, and barely realized. And he followed her and swam side by side with her, and presently he observed without alarm that others were in the water with them, like her, enough to have been her full sibs. So, then, the land was—or, smiling to himself as he conned the thought, at least the river was—not after all without inhabitants.

They seemed not alarmed by his being so different from them—he so rough, so much pelt, and they all so smooth and silvery. They smiled her same calm faint smile, swam slow circles round and round about them, he and she.

There seemed some faint disturbance in the water ... in the air ... he heard and felt a wind start up, heard suddenly a multitude of sounds ... looked up, looked back, and saw with a slow coldness in his loins and limbs that they were all quite close to him, they were almost touching him, they seemed about to dash at him. They were not smiling now and they were changed, greatly all were changed, yet clearly still he recognized them: their jaws were long and their teeth were sharp and still they gleamed silvery with red-brown glints and in that moment when all motion ceased he saw them truly for what they were.

Saw them to be undines, all of them, salmon-folk, the eternal enemies of the salmon-eating bear.

Their skins had been near them in this water all the time, but his was far away, so far away, on land, the land from which he heard clearly now that call which no fright nor chill could stay. Teeth flashed, they rushed—he leaped, caught the shadow which was the overhanging branch, stayed not to watch lest he lose all sway and fall back in, and heedless of roughed skin made his way upside down along the branch till he could be sure there was land beneath.

There on the bank not a hundred steps away stood Corm. The sun was very far down the sky— how could he have been in the water this long?—the sun was not warm at all upon him now. Corm's cheeks were distended and he wound the great fey

177

horn, and the sky sounded with the trumpet of the great swans and all multitudes of birds, and elk and red stags belled in the woods, the foxes barked and all creatures sang and sounded.

Arn walked, he staggered, he saw Corm see him and the calling ceased and he walked forward on his knees, only now feeling in loins and all his limbs shaken with sudden gusts of feeling. He saw the dark outline on the grass and he fell forward and laid his hands upon the bearskin.

It was not that day but the next day that he sat between the shallows and the deeps and slew the salmon by the score.

Chapter XIV

Roke laughed and then for a moment the laughter seemed about to turn into some other, infinitely less-pleasant sound, then it was once more a laugh. Long he laughed, and loudly, throwing back his head and sticking his chest out. Between the river and the steam-bath and the soapy herb old Bab had found and prepared and which all had used, all were clean now, but Roke seemed at that moment cleaner than any. His hair, which had grown dark and matted, was again light and the ends of it waved in the wind. Ugly reddled marks were still on his skin, but already much faded from when last they had seen them. And the red mark of the Star Bear glistened on his breast.

Eër-derred-derred-eër, who had never left Nainland before he had left with them, and so had never before seen smoothskins in full-exposed smoothness of skin, looked and wondered and opened his mouth as though he would laugh, too. His own shagginess was quite sleek and was lighter than the familiar chestnut-brown of the older nains. "Tall Roke, why do thee so much laugh?" he asked.

And Roke, who had finished with a prolonged silent spasm, lifted his well-worn leathers and sniffed at them, threw them down with a loud snort. "They have a half-winter's stink!" he said. "I shall hang them in a good safe tree to air well till we return, and my advice as friend and brother is for all of thee to do the same: else I must walk upwind. Yes! Naked I shall go, but I shall not stink— What ask, nain-fellow?—But although it be good to be feeling the clean wind all over clean me for a change, have I not got some clean garments of pounded bark-cloth?" He muttered and turned as though to go and open his pack, then turned again.

He faced the young nain and stared at him as though trying to think of either answer or question. Then his skin reddened until the Star Bear almost vanished and the red stain swept down until it vanished in the tangle of blonde hair. Then it ebbed. "I laughed, nainfellow, because there be a-many who deem me dead." And he told him why and how. "I laughed because until now I had very much doubted the fact of my dying, but until now I was perhaps not all sure, do 'ee see, shagfellow? And I laughed because I now know that I be in no wise dead, and I laughed to learn that though I did stink, it was a live man's stink and not a dead one's!"

He found his clean clothes, unrolled and stepped into them. They were all marked in root and berry-dye with a multitude of bright signs and sigils, suns and moons and stars and leaping stags and such-like. He patted and smoothed them, then straightened up until he was again for true Tall Roke. No trace of slouch or strain seemed to remain. And something had rolled off his soul as well.

"Now," he said, placing one hand upon the others' shaggy shoulder. "Do thee and me and two others follow the Bear and his witchery-hide-map and let us on to Wizardland and there us shall persuade mayhap several sages that they be n't dead, either!"

The Bear had also benefited by the several days of crouching in the steam-hut whilst water was dashed on red-hot stones and then rushing, streaming with sweat and sweated-loose winter-dirt, into the river. They had beaten each other with small bundles of twigs and sluiced themselves with soaproot, rubbed themselves and each other with sand and scraped their skins with flat stones and then they had done it all over again. The bear-skin had also been subject to a milder cleansing, and now dangled, inside-out over Arn's back, *flip*, *flap* it said as he stalked along. Had the Bear also benefited by anything else which had occurred by the river? Certainly he had benefited by the second sounding of All-Caller. As for more than that—

But the flapping of the bearhide reminded him of another hide, and he drew out the map the nains had painted for him. There was the green wiggle

180

and fish which meant *river*; they had passed that. Ahead was the sign for *fire*, repeated several times: how far ahead and exactly what this meant, he did not know. He understood that there were *hills* ... or was that, were they *mountains?* Did it at all matter?—it might. And over here, *this* odd sign meant *wizards*.

But, this one, this one, *this* one—? He slowed his pace and let the others catch up with him, then asked. He had expected that neither Corm nor Roke would know, and, indeed, though he had tried to explain the notion of a map to them, neither could form any other idea than that the hide was painted with witchery-signs: potent, yes: but not to be understood by them. Thus he was not surprised that when he indicated the sigil with his thumb the two of them merely breathed more deeply, and then looked at him.

His old uncle's dark brows, flecked with a few writhing white hairs, seemed themselves to gaze, as well as his eyes. He looked intently at the indicated sign. He said, "I may have known. I do not know now. But even those I know are not painted just as I would paint them, these be nain-paints, my sister's grandson."

Eër-derred-derred-eër looked long and looked close. "It says to me that once I did see it." He paused and looked more and, as he inclined his head, seemed indeed to listen as well as look. "It says no more," he concluded.

Arn sighed. Roke had thought of something. "Bab, why does thee not build a hut and make witchery over this sign, then?" And Arn made a pleased sound. But Bab slowly and emphatically shook his head.

"I do not know this sign," he repeated. "If I draw it, I may give it power. If I knew it, then I would know, for a first thing, how to keep power over it while I worked with it; and, if I knew it, then I would be able to obtain power from it ... perhaps. But to do witchery-work with a strange and unknown sign? No, Bear, and no, Roke: this is not done."

Roke drew away from the map, and, indeed, he would never draw near whenever it was open, again. And so they went on. The trees now were larch and spruce and aspen—not, as he had first thought, birch. And this once more put him in mind of the undines, and he wondered again what would have happened if Bab, alarmed at his not having returned by late afternoon, had not taken the major measure of telling Corm to blow the great fey horn. Twice, now, had it—they—saved him. He thought about this as they crossed the low, rolling hills carpeted with spring flowers; and then his mind fell into a reverie and he was not really aware what he was thinking of at all. Perhaps, then, he, least of any was prepared for that incident which brought from the nain a grunt of surprise, from Bab an exclamation of astonishment, from Roke a cry of alarm, and from Corm a wail of sheer pain.

Corm had set his foot down on it; he had been going slow, perhaps even dawdling, for he did not casually bring his foot up to take another slow step but stood there—not even holding it in his hand— stood there awkwardly on one foot, the other

182

merely suspended. And he pointed, his wail ending abruptly, subsiding into a hiss of anguish.

For where his foot had been was a small smoldering place in the grass. "Oh, it hurts!" he exclaimed. And hopped on one foot a pace to sit down and nurse his burn. They gathered round, partly to console and think what comfort they might administer, partly to examine this oddity. Their shadows fell across the tiny spot, and in that darkness they saw a small red eye of fire. Roke was first to speak.

"Make water on it," he said, "same as though 'twere a cut, for a man's own water has healing salts." This was customary folk-wisdom, all nodded, finding comfort in the known in face of the unknown. Roke helped Corm to his good foot, and, the younger man, leaning against him for support, began to carry out the suggestion; Roke himself followed his own counsel, but aimed his urine on the burning place. It hissed as though itself in pain, it steamed. And Bab rummaged in his bag of medicines and came up with a small horn of some fat a long-ago winter's night prepared with herbs. He murmured as he wiped Corm's foot dry with a tuft of grass and with his finger he gently spread the salve upon the already-reddening place, and fastened a very soft strip of bark around the foot from instep to sole; and fastened it so, deftly.

"Tis odd, tis odd," he murmured. "Tis very odd."

And then, Corm placing his weight upon the foot with only a slight grimace and they starting off once more, Arnten, pointing, said, "And not that one 'odd' alone: look—"

183

Ahead of them yet another wisp of smoke ascended.

They came up to it very cautiously, yet not so close as to the first one, yet it needed not that closeness, for it was somewhat larger. "It be a fire-ring," the young nain said. And sure enough, it was not a mere spot or small full-circle, but a true ring, and in the midst of the burning was an unburned core of grass.

"The grass is not dry," said Arnten.

"Well for us that it is not," his old uncle declared. "Else all might burn, and us with it." And they shuddered, remembering the great grass fires which sometimes swept the dry plains, driving men and beasts and birds before it in full terror and flight. Then, seeing Roke again fumbling at himself, "Nay, let us press on, thee cannot hope to piddle out every unsought smolder-fire we may meet—"

They laughed, perhaps more than the wit of it deserved, and they walked on, walked on faster. Then before their eyes and even while they scanned the turfy grass, they saw the next circle spring up into fire before their gaze. One united sound of dismay they made. Corm, as though without thinking, made a twisting movement with his index finger and began a childhood chant familiar to them all ... perhaps even to the nain. "*Ringy-ringy-ringworm, firey-firey-fireworm, little-worm, big-worm, out-thee-GO—!*"

At GO, he flung his finger out as though flicking something away. And they all solemnly spat three times, as though they were indeed children at solemn play trying to exorcize an itch.

"May it be to some avail, and soon," Bab said. "But let us not wait here to see, for while we have waited, there has another sprung up—" They started off at great pace, going off their straight-intended path to avoid this newer and, alas, greater circle of smoke and fire. And while they walked so quickly they, with one unspoken accord and one unrehearsed movement, looked back over their shoulders, as though to see if safety might be had by return.

Yet behind them as before them the gouts of fire on several sides were springing up, not less behind than before. They skirted this newest, nearest burning ring, and glanced away from it with some wordless noises of satisfaction, but pleasure was short-lived indeed: for whilst they were circling one circle, all round and round about them another one had been growing.

They broke into a run, they raced as never Arnten had remembered racing, not even when he had fled from the sudden mob in his home hamlet; and they did not pause, they leaped over the low-smouldering loop; and landed, half-stumbling, half-falling, on the yonder side. For a moment, at least, safety.

But fire-loop was now crossing and intersecting fire-loop, and though they kept on running, kept on jumping and kept on leaping, there was no more sign of reaching unburning land than there seemed to be of the medicine-chant's having had any success. Arnten's pack humped and bumped and flapped against his side, and he made a ducking gesture so as to pass the belt over his head and so let the pack drop and so be rid of it and so run on the faster and the better: in drawing the pack up past his face, or in drawing his face down past his pack, his nostrils were met with a wet and musty smell, almost a stink, a reek of something which was not fish, though for an instant he thought of that; nor yet snake, though for a second he was reminded of that. There was something very important, urgent, in that brief reek. His mind said: Run! His feet said: On! His heart said: Woe!

But his nose said, Stop!

And he stopped, and surrounded as he was by heat and by reek and by smoke and by the smoking shadows of death, down he sat him. He heard say, moaning, "Arnten has fallen—"

Roke: "Arnten? Back, then, back to him—"

The nain came trotting and came shambling back, not fearing now to let himself be seen on all his four limbs, his long arms, knuckles to ground, aiding him as though legs; the nain made his way with surprising swiftness, and he took hold and Arnten flung his arm off— "Eh, a-be's daft, 's brains do turn from fear and fire!" the nain bellowed, and made as though to catch him up and carry him off. Arnten, burrowing in his pack, delving and tugging, brought up his sweat-streaked face, forced himself to speak.

"I am not—" he panted. He thrust up a hand to avoid Roke's lunging arm.

"My mind is well—" he ducked to escape his uncle's withered paw.

"Don't leave me— wait, wait—for you—for you as well for me—here—here—here—and here—"

At full long last he had it from his pack, he had the packet, he had it unfastened, he spread it out, unfolding it. He gestured, he tried to explain, his voice breaking. Half they would seize and drag him, half they strove to get his meaning. Half they would have fled and saved themselves, half they were full loathe to do so. And it was, as might have been expected, Bab, who first comprehended.

Who stooped, snatched up, sat himself down. Who cried, doing so, "That sign ... that witchery sign ... Nay, bind your feet, all! Bind your feet! Wrap these strips of skin round about your feet! These be the cutting from that beast back there, from that dragon-beast, from that salamander ..."

And they sat themselves down, though death was burning brightly all round about them. And they gravely wrapped around their feet the wet and cold skin of the salamander, the dragon, the dead dragon, finding their life in his death. And they arose, and with one's hand on the other's shoulder, coughing and stumbling in the smoke, they strode yet safely across the burning rings. And nothing of them did burn.

Chapter XV

Wizardland looked fey indeed.

It seemed as though many great rivers, or one great river which had shifted its channel repeatedly, had coursed through the land over endless ages. Eroded cliffs, gaunt escarpments, high and low plateaus and buttes were the up-and-down features of the terrain. Grey gravel crunched under their feet, and then there was grey sand and then smooth grey pebbles which were hard for feet to find a purchase on, rolling and sliding. This gave way to wide beds of coarse red sand and beyond that the red sand was finer and then their trudging, stumbling feet sent up clouds of red dust which bit into nostrils and throat. The way led between huge black boulders beneath beetling black cliffs and nut-sized black pebbles graded slowly into seed-sized grains of black sand which hissed beneath their feet. After a while there were streaks of gold in the blackness, and then streaks of blackness in the floor of golden sands. Black and white and gold and black and red, over and over again.

But of the river or rivers which had, ages after ages, rolled and roared and ground and eaten into the tortured surface of the land, eaten their way deeper and deeper, eaten the rock into gravel and the gravel into sand, washing away every trace of soil, leaving not even a pocket of true earth—of these mighty and age-long waters, not a drop remained. The courses of Wizardland were dry, long dry.

The courses of Wizardland were dry.

Witchery-Bab crooned a soft song, chanting in the Old Tongue. In each hand he held a branch of rowan with the red berries dried on them. The others had spread out from him without speaking, almost without thinking of it.

When the old man paused, as he did now and then, they all did the same. Now, to the right, an enormous black spire of rock retreated upward at a shallow slant. Vast and irregular red-and-black streaked blocks lay to the left as though tumbled and left there by giants at play. A slight wind rustled the rowan twigs in the old man's hands and the berries rattled. But there was no wind felt upon them, however slight. Only a chill, a crawling of the skin, a puckering of flesh around erect hairs, as they saw the rowans tremble and move in the old man's hands, and slowly and slowly shift.

And the old man shifted with them till they ceased to shift further, only they trembled and the dried berries rattled on the dried twigs. And the old man moved on, and they moved on with him.

A canyon of grey rocks all humble-tumble and eaten into a wilderness of holes prepared them gradually for the great inward-slanting cleft in the rock which they saw before them at the time of no shadows, at the canyon's end. A blind wall of high grey stone faced them, blind, that is, save for the single slant eye of the cavern. And they slumped, all, and stopped, all, and all of them sighed what seemed to be one same and drawn-out sigh.

Now for the first time since they had entered this fey region of rock and sand and cliff and stone, the old man seemed to be slightly uncertain as to what move he must make next, and he stood hesitant, his mouth moving but his song silent, and the rowan twigs still rustling in his hands. In his old uncle's eyes as they now turned towards him, Arnten read the wish for help. He took two strides and took the rowans and set them flat upon the smooth grey sands of the canyon floor, straightly pointing to the cavern mouth. There was a slight sound in his throat as the medicine-twigs slithered forward the space of the breadth of a few fingers, as though drawn by hands unseen. Then they stopped. A dry susurration as of insects' wings seemed to sound all round them in the dry, flat air: but if it was still an actual sound or the memory of one, the faces which they wore implied nought but doubt.

Next Arnten merely dropped his burden, and this heavy and simple sound, accompanied by the relieved grunt of a man simply glad to be lighter of a weight, changed the mood. For all of them bore burdens, and they all now hasted to let them slide as they stooped and turned. The old one groped and fumbled his fire-kit, made no objection when Roke, with a murmur, squatted beside him and took up the sticks and the dried fungus and plied his hands rapidly to work. Now Arn and nain-Eër set to work to cut the thigh-bone of the deer from the hip-socket and the flesh of the haunch from the bone, stone knife and iron knife and force and thrust and snap and slash. The liver and a slab of the kidney fat lay neatly wrapped together in a deer pouch.

Fire spurted soon from the pinches of dried fungus fed into the socket of the lower fire-stick, moved to a handful of rush grass, was fed to a cone of thin sticks, ate the heavier firewood they had brought upon their backs to this land devoid of twig or grass or tree ... died down into coals. The marrow bone was laid in first to roast, and then the liver and the fat, which fed the fire its own unctuous fuel without the need of more wood. The spittle filled their dried mouths, but none dared as yet even lick a finger.

And still and always the echo of a dry rustling seemed to sound in every ear.

Arnten presently cracked open the steaming marrow-bone and he poked out the soft marrow-core and let it fall upon the clean piece of bark which did for dish. And next to it he set a slice of the crisped fat, and beside that he placed a slice of the liver, bubbling richly in its blood.

"Salt," he said.

They gave him the bone bottle of sea-salt and he opened the carved stopple and sprinkled the offering with the clean white crystals, six times strained through fine filters. Then he rose to his feet and the bark platter was carefully handed up to him and he and the old man walked with deliberate pace forward, and the others sat where they were, and trembled. And the two walked into the cave and then their feet were heard and then their feet were not.

The adjustment from light to shadow was gradual, and in the half-light they saw something protruding from the wall of the inner cave which might have been a mummy-bundle, all grey and dusty and clad in wrappings: but mummy-bundles do neither tremble, howsoever faintly, nor do they twitch and rustle. Recognitions came in quick flashes. Two bundles of twigs: hands. Faint gleams as of dew-light on dirty stones: eyes. Ceremonial mask long hung away forgotten, to moulder and gather dust: face. The faint drone, faint rustlings, the faint movements were reminiscent of nothing so much as of the tired and desperate and hopeless motion and sound of an insect somehow still faintly alive in winter.

Arnten first dipped his finger in the bubble-blood

and poked it into the dry, dry cavern of the mouth, felt it touch the dry and dusty, faintly trembling tongue. The travesty of a mouth with the least conceivable pressure sucked the seethed blood from the fingertip as though a newborn and dying babe were sucking milk from a teat. Next he smeared the fat of the offering upon the dry, seared lips, the sear cracked lips; and watched them slowly close upon each other, heard the almost inaudible smack of those dead and dusty lips. He wafted the odorous steam of the meal under those dust-choked nose holes. He saw the grey-smeared eyelids quiver, the faint gleam widen.

So, slowly, slowly, slowly, he fed the wizard.

The first thing the wizard said, after a long time: *"Now, my sibs there ..."* Even farther into the shadow and the gloom were two other huddled bundles which buzzed and rustled like two dying flies; Arnten perceived how close alike is life's revival to its conclusion.

So, slowly, slowly, slowly, he fed the wizards.

They ate the liver, every morsel. They sopped up the marrow, every soft crumble of it. They licked up every congealing drop of fat. By this time it was so far declined from noon, when he had entered, that he could barely make out their nodding heads and wavering hands as they dismissed him. "It was well done," he was told, in creaking, faltering tones. "And now we would rest a moment, till the daylight come again."

The empty piece of bark, which Arnten burned upon the barely-living fire, answered the question his companions did not ask. He and his old uncle and counsellor sank down and sighed heavy signs and watched the greasy bark, once clean, blaze brightly in the dying embers. They blinked. After a while Arnten asked, "Have you eaten?"

There was a somewhat incredulous silence. And Corm asked, "Have *you*?"

"We? We were feeding wizards . . ." Now it was the turn of Corm, Roke, and Eër-derred-derred-eër to sigh.

"Feeding wizards," the young nain repeated. He paused. The great part of their journey had been accomplished; for—it seemed to him now—all his life he had been hearing his elders and even his age-peers muttering "The wizards must be fed"; that, were they but fed, the curse would vanish from iron, the king and the kingsmen would cease to molest, that the forges of Nainland once again would grow hot and their smokes attaint the air: once again all would be as before; hence, all would be well. But now Nainland seemed infinitely far away, and its concerns infinitely remote. In this arid and barren land only one thing now seemed real to him—his hunger. And although his tongue still retained some natural diffidence, his body did not.

The young nain's enormous and unpremeditated eructation echoed in the all but complete darkness and rolled from canyon wall to wall. For a moment Corm and Roke waited, aghast, for some ghostly wizard, or some wizardly ghost, to avenge the insult. But the echoes died away, and all, for the moment, was silent—but only for a moment. Next Corm's belly gave a series of warning rumbles, and then from his mouth, too, for a second, blowing aside the wispy moustaches and beard which now proudly obscured it, broke the same impatient sound which had from the nain's. And next and at once, as though rehearsed, and well-rehearsed, a by far deeper series of growls caused Roke's taut belly to writhe, and he uttered by far the loudest brunk of the three.

Old Bab slowly and economically laid a twig at the edges of the fire. It fired. He showed what might have been a small old smile on those lips which none there had ever really seen to smile before.

"I wit it not," said Arnten, slowly shaking his head. "The wizards alone have eaten, all three, and now you three here— Eh. Well." He reached for the carcass of the deer, drew it towards him and the fire. "Well. Eh. Now, then, do we let eat. And let the wizards . . ." His voice died away. And presently the drip-drip-drip of fat into the fire caused it to spurt and flare. And Wizardland saw and heard a feast which was neither magic nor symbolic. And afterwards they let the fire die down, and then they all lay near the ashes. And slept.

In the morning an odd and unfamiliar droning sound they heard, but, being both bone-weary and full of meat, they grunted and rolled over and covered their eyes against the interfering sun. The droning increased, became clamorous. They sat bolt upright, all of them. A clear sunlight shone cleanly on the grey sands and grey stones of this canyon in Wizardland. Three figures they saw before them, now standing still, now walking back and forth, now gravely folding their legs under

194

them and sitting, now sedately rising to their feet and waving their arms and now turning their backs, and then at once turning to face them again.

It was the three wizards of the caves, well-awakened from their long and hungry slumbers, and giving tongue and voice to the comments and the conversation and the thoughts and dreams, the unanswered and, indeed, the unasked questions of a hundred years tumbling from their lips—lips no longer sere and cracked but full and red, eyes no longer dull under dusty eyelids but gleaming bright. And mouths no longer dry, and certainly no longer choked with dust and certainly no longer silent. The wizards of Wizardland—at least three of them—had been fed. And these three wizards of Wizardland were now speaking. All at the same time. And they spoke and they spoke and they spoke, and they walked as they spoke and they spoke as they walked.

For three days and for three nights, during which the five companions first looked and listened with astonishment and then with awe, and next tried to sort out any syllables from any other syllables, and at first with diffidence and then with desperation and after that with something close to wrath and then with growing bafflement tried to be heard themselves . . .

For three days and for three nights the three wizards talked without ceasing and walked as they talked, back and forth. Then as it approached the cold grey dawn when the ghosts all flee, a gradual silence fell. And the walking slowed. And, one by one, with an abrupt but not ungraceful movement each, the wizards sat them down and stayed seated.

195

Red-eyed, not sure if they themselves were asleep or awake, or perhaps doomed to remain and gather dust for a century, weary and confused and not certain of anything, the five watched in silence.

And then the nearest of the wizards, and evidently the one first fed, said in a clear tone, unfatigued, "Men and man-Bear and youngling nain. You have fed us sufficedly, you have listened to us not unpatiently, and you are waiting for us unhastily. This is all according to the natural order and basis of things—and far different—we perceive—from a former age which allowed us to famish: ahah ahah ahah! *That* was not well done! Anumph. We dwell not on that. We have waited and you have waited, and although your wait was not so long as ours, think not that we exact hour for hour. Nay. So. One at a time, then, speak you speaking and we shall hearken. And ask, for here eventually come all answers, undistracted by the false delights of life such as be in other lands and provinces, such as fruits and trees and fair flowers and female flesh and wild beasts and birds for to hazard and for to chase: but here be ne things but stone and sand and clean pure air ... and, of course, anumph, we the wizards ... Therefore, all wisdom cometh here and all knowledge cometh here and all writings and wottings and all sapiences and powers. To be sure that they adventure forth from their sources and disperse over every land and province and island and main, but in thother places there be such distractions as I did mention priorly, hence all wisdom there does dissipate and all knowledge doth melt and doth dwindle ...

"But the spirit and ghost of all thought and

learning cometh here in their comings and find ne thing to disadvantage them, and hence we of the wizardry do absorb them as we absorb a sunbeam. Nought do distract us, neither getting nor giving nor delving nor tilling nor trapping nor chasing, of neither kind of venery are we attracted, and we hew no wood, having none to hew. Hence all these wisdoms and wittings and wottings do accumulate amongst us and are but diminished in the very slightly by that we do one time in an undren yearen eat one meal. And if towards the conclusion of that cycle cometh another meal, we scruple ne to eat it also. And if there cometh none, we do but estivate and wait.

"However, we account it as an ill-done thing if none of the folk who dwell in the world of fleshly forms take pain to bring us not so much as a suppance of blood, liver, fat and marrow, sprinkled lightly with clean sea-salt and served as is proper upon a clean piece of bark, not e'en one time in one undren yearen. To speak as to the point, as be our manner, sparingly and sparsingly and without a superfluity of syllables this neglectancy hath disturbed the pure concentrations in which we would prefer to spend our days and times and cycles, it hath happed—that we can recall—but a two or a three times since men began to dwell upon the soil of Ultima Thule, and as for the other Thules and what did and did not occur in those lands and in those days, we chuse not now to speak.

"Who in general hath sent us food but the kings who have set their feet upon the necks of men? For who else hath had power to summons men from fireside and women's arms and send them upon the journey hither, the distances and perils of which men have alway so exaggerated, as though a swamp or a salamander or a what or a which were all that much matter or marvel? Well, well, it be not for us to bear grudge or execute vengencies; but if the generalty be not reminded they will themselves suffer, thus out of a concern for them greater than our concern for ourselves, we have found it needful and necessary to set forth a doom. No doubt this doom hath vexed a king and he hath been moved to enquire as to what uncare of which natural basis and order of things hath upset the universal balencies. Anumph. Anumph."

This wizard had the form of a man in full vigor, with ruddy cheeks and sparkling eyes. And the second wizard bore the form of a stripling youth and smiled and cast down his face as it seemed he were shy in such a company, and spoke so softly that the others strained to hear. "Wethinks that we've slumbered longer than somewhile, as usual," he murmured. "Weseems it be arrived to the near time of Fireborn, the first-born son of Fire, who hath so often died and ever returned in one form or another. Ah we, but have ever born a love for Fireborn, and would gladly go forth even from our choicest place of wizardry for to see and for to be with Fireborn again ..." His words passed from words into a sound like the laughter of a stripling young man who deems it delicate not to behave too vigorously in the presence of elders.

The third wizard had the form of a stout witchery-woman and sage femme, a granny of good wealth and position and hale, yet in all her health and humors, with a dignified sprinkling of beard upon her face, and she pursed her lips and said in the tone of one giving portents, *"One queen is every queen, beware,"* and it seemed to Arnten that he had heard this once, and that certainly to hear it twice and elsewhere and moreover from such a source enhanced it as a caution: but for the moment he could not pause to consider it, but he placed it into his memory as a squirrel does a nut in its cheek or an ox a cud in her rumen. And she said, *"When the stars throw down their spears and pelt the earth with thunderstones, go seek the new iron to cure the old."* And she said these things with a heavy and a slow tone, rolling her eyes and bobbing her head heavily.

The first wizard had spoken so profusely and so swiftly, as though still making up for more than a century of not speaking at all, that he had almost lost them. And the second wizard had spoken so softly that almost they had not heard him at all. But now the manner of the third wizard was so familiar to them, and her voice neither too swift nor too soft: and so they listened full well.

And she told them, "There is come an end to certain things, and thus a beginning to certain others," and they nodded. And she said, "The wood which has burned without burning shall be fittest to burn for Fireborn," and they leaned forward and missed no syllable. And she spoke of many another thing, but the two things she had said first stirred most in the mind of Arnten.

And he bethought him, even as he listened, what it might mean: *One queen is every queen,* and he thought that somehow he did know. And he wondered how *The stars* could indeed *throw down their spears and pelt the earth with thunderstones*, and he knew that this he did not know at all.

But must wait until the knowing of it would be revealed.

Chapter XVI

The name of the first wizard, they learned, was Gathonobles. And the name of the second was Wendolin. And the name of the third was Immaunya. And it was the second who accompanied them.

Arnten was not sure by any means that they had learned all that he would know, but they could not stay; there was no food in Wizardland save that which they had brought with them; nor any water or other drink, either. So the five were now increased to six, and the two other wizards they saw, as they went their way from the grey canyon walled with grey time-eaten stones and floored with grey time-washed sand, still sitting and pondering; no longer engaged in talk, no longer paying their visitors any mind at all: but sitting as they might sit another hundred years, absorbing the thoughts of all the outside worlds.

As surely as they knew that each night the sun descended, stained and tired, to be refreshed and refurbished in the fires of Lower Hell, so they knew that their new companion was older by far than any living man was old, perhaps older than calculation. But they knew it as men know a thing which belongs to the realm of wisdom, as, for one, men know that to lie with a strange woman and spend one's seed in her is bad, because with this seed she may make strong and malign witcheries: but as for the spontaneous sense of the moment, one knows that to lie with a woman and to spend one's seed in her is good. So, by wisdom, they knew that Wendolin was a wizard, and very old; but only Arntenas-Arnten had seen him as a barely viable bundle in the cave, and even he would need strain to acknowledge that the Wendolin who moved and walked and shyly smiled among them was that same being. Nor did he strain. Nor did the wisdom fact remain forever and always in their minds: they had seen him as a stripling lad, thus they saw him now, he did not change before their eyes, and so he did not change in their minds.

And on this subject once old Bab said to his great-nephew, "There must be some deep reason why his shape and semblance is thus: and I incline to think that tis because this is his real nature."

And no more was said or thought on it. Wendolin had no beard upon his face, but then, till recently, neither had Corm; this did not distinguish him in any ill sense, and neither did his grey-green eyes, his somewhat dark countenance, his clothes of russet leather. From what beast his clothes had come, or who had gathered the bark to tan them, or when, none of them to be sure knew. But then, no one cared. "I know a quicker way out," he said, easily, in his clear, free voice. And they were glad that he did, and they followed him without concern. His words proved true; he led them through a cleft in the gaunt grey cliffs, out into the nameless

201

land of woods and grass and streams which lay aside to Wizardland. And they breathed a relieved breath, and smiled on him, and touched his arm. His own smile was a trace less shy. He was now one of them, it seemed. And all had an unspoken feeling that their number was now complete.

And they killed game, and ate of it, and they ate of fruit and berries and of greens.

It was as they stood by a stand of berry-canes, with no great thought upon them more than to avoid the thorns, that one clear and distant sound came to their ears, and then Roke grew a bit white, and he lay his hands upon his scars. And for a moment the blood of the berries seemed as though it were his own blood.

He said, "That is surely the voice of Spear-Teeth. Am I to go and kill him now? Or to be killed by him again, this time for true and ever? Does no one know?"

Carefully they snuffed up the breeze, as though the faint sound they made in doing so would be heard, and to their danger. And over the green scent of growing things there lay the heavy and dangerous must-smell of the great mammont. And they were all still, the berries still between the cusps of their teeth.

"Oh, perhaps neither of those," said Wendolin. "I think it is none of those," he said, his manner seeming easy, though somewhat grave. His trifle smile slightly spread his red lips. "But before this Bear and I go to see what Big One has to say to us, I think," he said, softly but not fearfully, "I think we will eat some more good berries. It is long since I have eaten such," he said. And his manner as he stripped the withes was as simple and hearty as that of any boy who feasts himself with berries after a long dearth of them. And Arnten did the same.

Slowly the whiteness in Roke's face diminished. He looked at his new friend all clad in russet with some slight surprise and admiration. "Then I am not to see him now," he said, low-voiced, and slightly indistinct. He moved his tongue and seemed bemused to find berry mashed upon it, and he swallowed. "Mmmm ... It be a different thing for thee, Wendo," he said—for he had spoken of his incomplete dying, and all of that, earlier. "Eh, thee may stand beside him and eat berries and wail thy weirds and stand safe indeed ... but as for me and as for he ... I feel that when the pair of us come sight to sight, and close, again, that one of us must soonly be dead for true and ever." He stood a moment. Then he moved. Said, "But as tis not to now, then now I'll do as Wendo says—I'll eat berries." And he gave a sudden snort of laughter and his head a good shake. And he ate more berries.

By and by, Arnten felt his body give a great impatient twitch and he grunted and laid his heavy hand as lightly on Wendolin's slight shoulder as he could, and gave him a little push. Wendolin with a rueful, laughing look, but with no word, reached for one last, large berry, did not reach to it, and so the two of them departed from the rest.

The great roan mammont trumpeted when he saw them emerge out of the bosque, and swung round, shambled off. The open ground was broken and irregular, and often he was out of sight. Once they over-walked a tuft of his fleece upon a thornbush, and once they by-passed a huge pile of his steaming dung. Once the wind shifted and they paused, and he sounded again, as though impatiently, and they followed in the direction of his call.

Arnten asked, "Have you also received the thoughts of Spear-Teeth?"

"Oh yes."

"What are they like?"

"Mostly they are heavy and hairy. And sometimes they are steamy and dungy."

Arnten rumbled a laugh in his big, shaggy chest. It did seem a somewhat strange to be following after the great mammont, instead of trying to avoid it; and they did not even intend to try to kill it. But the strange was now the usual, the usual had become so strange by former standards that ... that what? He sought a short thought to sum it all up, found none. He was like a man who settles into a steady run and no longer pauses to consider what a thing looks like when one slowly skulks around it. For years he had skulked around the events in life, well, that had not been his own choice; but now he was in effect running—though, in fact, he now at this moment walked—running with head thrown back and chest thrown out and feeling the wind and taking the wind in and feeling the growth and play of his muscles and the expansion of his thoughts.

"This would have been his mate," said Wendolin. There was nothing to show them what had caused this other mammont's death—or, if there was, Arnten did not observe nor Wendolin point out. But beasts had gnawed clean its bones, and it must have been a long and ample feast for them. And there were even teeth marks on the stump of tusk which protruded from the socketed skull on the upper side. "Not this," said Wendolin. His hands brushed aside grasses, found something barely sticking above the surface of the ground, said, pointing, "This. Take it up, brother."

Arnten reached, seized, tugged, grunted, drew forth the lower end of the dead mammont's tusk.

"'*This*' . . . ?"

Wendolin had already turned and started back. He said, without turning, "That is for Fireborn. His haft."

The others marvelled and murmured much on seeing the ivory. But he all clad in russet merely smiled shyly and crammed his mouth with berries.

One other new thing stayed much in Arnten's mind. On another day, and days later, when they had begun to see from time to time the rising smokes of men's places, and turned wide aside to avoid them—he and Wendolin had gone off again together, and then Arn had begun to think deep, bearish thoughts. After a while he saw that he was alone, and so sank back into his thoughts. Then slowly rose from them again. Heard faint voices. Odd sounds. There seemed a new strangeness in the air, scents familiar and yet not so. Walking softly, softly, he saw Wendolin in the soft grasses, bare of skin, arms and legs spread out upon the ground. Yet stranger: Wendolin seemed to have doubled, for, beneath him, and very next to the grassy ground, was a second Wendolin: one, face down;

one, face up: face to face, arms to arms, body to body, legs to legs.

As Arn stood in full astonishment, the lower face twisted and one of the lower eyes turned and saw him. And at that the awesome stillness of the scene was shattered and the lower body struggled its way out from the upper, there was a scramble of limbs, a body leaped to its feet and Arnten saw it was that of a woman, with visible breasts. *Is Wendolin, then—?* His mind groped for understanding. Then, as one body fled, still silent, the other turned over and it met his eyes and it laughed a little. *It* was Wendolin; *this* was Wendolin. Smiling his still slightly shy smile and without haste or shame or alarm, he reached slowly for his clothes. "When I am among men," he said, "I do as men do." And, indeed, he was made full as other men be made.

Many thoughts rocketed like startled birds in Arnten's mind. He felt a host of urges, changes starting in his flesh, and almost he turned to pursue after the fled girl. Then he asked, "Do you not fear, then, that when your seed flows from her she will take some upon a leaf or two and save it away in her witchery-things for working a later malevolence upon you?"

"No," said Wendolin, shortly and easily, sliding his legs into his breeches. His smile he stowed away and faced Arnten face to face. "And neither need you," he said.

"This I will remember," said Arnten slowly. Later on he would reflect and endeavor to find out if this meant that no men need really fear such a thing (when all men he knew did indeed fear it), or if he, Arnten, by virtue of his bearhood or his wizard-friend's remark, need not. But now he said, "Then what of this as has been heard by me more than once, that *One queen is every queen*—"

"Ah, that is quite a different thing. Beware, indeed, of queens, for indeed, one queen *is* every queen. And yet, though every queen be a she, not every she be a queen ..."

He was clothed now and as before, except for a flush in his cheek and a sparkle in his eye, and—yes—his lips were fuller, redder; Wendolin said, "But only, friend, *Beware*. Not to tremble, nor forget your strength nor wisdom, but merely to beware. Be wary."

And Arnten, still strongly confused by new thoughts and things, not understanding by half or half of half, slowly repeated, "This I will remember."

Chapter XVII

Arnten knew that all were cautious on his behalf, knew it and knew it to be well that they were. For him and for his cause they had all, in part at least, left the known for the unknown and the secure for the perilous. And to the extent that they had not, to that extent they counted on him to bring better in the stead of worse. Did they not represent all the Land of Thule which was not represented by himself? "Our thing is the Thing of Thule: our matter is the Matter of Thule." In a way it be-

hooved him to be in the lead and for them to follow; in another way it behooved the others to pre-
cede him and be a-watch on his behalf for danger.

He could see both clearly, but he could not
clearly come to terms with both. As he felt himself
grow in bodily stature, so he believed with a certainty which was almost absolute that he was also
growing in experience and hence in wisdom as well.
And there were times when he had to be by himself, and it seemed he felt the need more and more
often, and it seemed, as well, the more he believed
it the less the others were willing to accord it him.

"To be cautious is one thing," he growled. "To
be fearful of being by yourselves, another." And
when he saw them gaze at him with distress upon
their faces and words upon their lips, he said,
flatly,—not least because he thought that perhaps
there might be in words a wise distress he cared not
to hearken to— "I am not to be followed. *Bide*,"
and was off, long strides, heavy and hairy arms
a-swing. And looked not back.

What was the plan? He would go and think upon
the plan and be free to mutter aloud, yes. What
plan? Would Fireborn come to him ... to them ...
piece by piece and bit by bit? Was he in some way
to urge, perhaps to force, or surely at least by some
act of his own purposefulness, to bring Fireborn to
him? He was tired of this drifting through the
wooded lands like a leaf among leaves. Hiding,
when he was ready for confrontation. Whispering,
when prepared for the shout of battle cry. Lurking,
slinking: when an increasing tremor in his heart
and blood shouted to him to rush forward. To rush
forward upon this lowbuilt and widespreading man-

sion suddenly now before him in the dark timbers of the wood, to impress himself upon and to make visible his mark, as footprints in dark sand, as a brand upon a hide or balk. An axe cleaving wood. Or cleaving flesh. To cleave, himself, the yielding flesh which waited for and sang to him.

Half his mind was turned, intent, into and upon itself the while he considered the mansion within the enclosure within the basky darkness of the dale; and half his mind considered only it and what might be inside, ignoring anything, everything else. He could not even recall at what moment he first had noticed it, or what thoughts first came to him concerning it. The guards and the thralls of whoever held the place moved to and from between house and wall and their livery was yellow and brown. He saw them moving vessels of drink, and his tongue and his throat moved; he watched them toting lugs of food, and his teeth champed and his belly growled. He saw the small spears and he scorned them. The man of this place was gone, he knew, he knew, he knew.

It was almost as though he had but stood tall and straight and planted his legs a-spread on the forest path and the house to him came swimming, the soft startled murmur of its folk subsiding as they all approached. He flexed his hands and waited for a spear to move his way, but the spearbearers bowed low before him. Servants walked backwards as he approached, gesturing him onward.

"Who keeps this place?" he asked.

"*Within*," they murmured, murmuring low: "*within, within, within.*"

He passed through many chambers and observed the industry of the thralls and the neatness and the richness of all.

"Whither do you take me?" he asked, in mock bemusement at the multitude of the rooms.

"*Within*," they murmured, murmuring low: "*within, within, within, within*."

Spearpoints down, they surrounded him; heads bowed low, they compassed him about. "*Without—*"

How sweet and rich this voice. How beautiful the gesture of her arm as she motioned to her guards and servantry to keep outside, and to him, to enter. Wide was this chamber indeed and dim and deeply scented and upon a divan upon a dais she reclined and slowly, slowly, arose, and she looked level eye to level eye at him as he approached. No slim sprig of a greenwood shrub was this, but a heavy bough all in fruit and all in flower. With gold and with amber was she adorned, and "Do you know me now?" she asked.

He bowed. "The Woman of the Woods, for true."

"You do," she said.

There were some men, if so one could or would call them, some several fat boys with lustrous eyes and sleek soft flesh, cowering and clustering about the dais. He looked at them one hot flash of a look and they, a-sulk, slunk away, taking care to tote away with them their furs and their sweets and their silky-softy gay array of robes: her loverboys. Ah well. Now he was here. Was it not time? Was it not time? Past time . . .

And she, as slowly she sank back and down

awaiting him, murmured, murmured, murmured low, low, low, ". . . be sparing of your teeth, your claws, be not swift to crush with your embrace, O Bear, O Bear, O Bear . . ."

His heart was like a mighty hammer upon a red-hot forge.

He heard the heavy blow and he felt the heat and he dimly saw her lift the stoup of mead for him to drink, as though to give him yet more sweetness and more zeal, as though either would be a-lack; he heard, he heard, he stooped his mouth to take the drink, his eyes did not leave hers, his hands groped for hers, he heard the wild swans and he heard their trumpets and he heard the bugles of the elks and the baying of the wild things abroad and he lifted his head in dread and saw the servants, saw the guards drawing close a-crouch with spears between their legs as though he might not see and he saw her a queen and he saw her as the queen of all the bees and he heard the raging murmur of her workers and her warriors and the faint death moans of her drones and he saw that she knew now that he knew and he dashed her honey-drink to the ground and he turned and struck out and fled and trampled and then he was without, he was outside, he was alone, he was not alone, he sobbed his frustrated lust and he sobbed his pain and he felt the stings and he saw the company of his friends and saw in their eyes relief and grief and saw All-Caller sink away from the distended cheeks of Corm—

"Why let not ye me—" he panted. "Have I not a right—?"

And overhead he heard, beyond his reach, the

bees, the bees, forever enemy of the bears, forever now to spy upon him, forever. The salmon dies after spawning, the were-salmon, undines; the lover-bee is stung to death, the death of the drone, after mating with the queenbee. *One queen is every queen . . .*

"Be not too fierce against us, Bear," said Roke, diffident and low, regretful. "Thy weird is not ours, ours is not thine: a merry dallying for us can be death for thee. Thy weird is otherwise, and the time of that for thee is not this . . . and not yet . . . not yet."

And that night he prepared himself for a dream and in that dream he saw what it was that he must do. Moon-dawn brightened the sky as he awoke and sought in the medicine-bundles for the things of need, and then he left them all wrapped in their pelts and in sleep, and his feet made no sound as they flatly pressed the earth and the grass already wet from the first dew, shining brightly in the light of the moon-maid's lamp. His eyes scanned grass for long and far and then he saw that heaped-up pile of it which signified his first stop. And he set his snares and he said his spells and he sat in the tree and he watched. And he waited. And he waited, and he watched.

"All hares are my hares," she said.
"And one queen does for all queens," he said.
"You think all ill of me . . ."
"Persuade me not to . . ."
She sat, her feet thrust under her again, all in blue. "You sought the hare. You caught the hare.

212

You set free the hare and you sent the hare to me, from you. In what way, then, have you yet to be persuaded?"

"In that way by which you think I think all ill of you."

"And again will that fey horn come soon a-sounding, to fill your ears with witchery and your eyes with witchery and send you fleeing me with fear and with rage and hate?"

He shook his head, his head all glowing with the drops of night, all glowing in the silver lamp. "He who sounds the horn and all of them lie sleeping still and will not wake till I bid them wake: but that same spell which keeps them sleep also keeps them safe."

"I desire nothing of them, nor ill nor well do I wish them."

He looked at her, ageless and cool, serene and without rage and he recollected whence she had come.

"Why have you sent for me?" she asked. "I am not used to being sent for, as well you must know."

Arnten said, "Clearly I cannot go to you with the same safety by which you came to me. It was not to glee myself with the thought of, 'Ah, and though she be whom she be, yet I did but send and she did come to me.' "

She said, "I know."

And so he knew that she did and he knew then that there was no need for any speech but the flat truth which lies at the base of all things without exception, in some cases to support them and in others to destroy them. And so he came somewhat closer and looked upon her grave beauty and he said, "I had begun to be the true me when I fled away from my childhood. And when I gained me the companions whom I now have, then I thought that they were also for me. And now increasingly I feel that they are for a something of which I am only a part, and this late time it has been seen by me that it is not enough. I feel like one dancing on a rope while a drum or tambour is tapped and rattled: though all look at him and though all laugh and applaud and though one who has never seen the sight may think that the Bear does dance because it is his wish, yet it is not so. And I have sent for you to see if we cannot cut this rope. For you in your way are also tied at a rope."

She said, "Yes."

She said, "And now I do see that it is one rope which ties us and which yet has kept us apart. Young for your father was I, and old for you be I: yet perhaps in neither case it need be so. He was much. He was great. Also, he was stubborn, he could not be moved more than can be moved some great stone boulder. Because you are younger you may be supple if you choose. I said to him, 'We do not need to stay and struggle. I have those ships of which you know and they have rich cargoes of which you know and they be at rest in that portlet and harbor of which you know. Let us twain depart and delight together and visit that other world which lies beyond Thule across the all-circling sea.' And he said: 'Delight indeed would that be. But my true delight will be to slay that wolf.' —Feel you so?"

He looked deep, deep into her eyes, said, "No." Said, "I cared nothing for that wolf, save that he

214

stood between me and my life. Then my father's death . . . But now of this late time I know that more important to me than my father's death is his son's life. And so it is that I have come to see that I may well have another life than this one of hunt and flee, of hide and sleep, of seek to slay. Now, and if I stripped that wolf's skin from off him. Now, and if I became King of Farthest Thule in the stead of him. Now, and of whom would I be king? Of them that stoned me, of them that bound me, of all them, being them who are as I am in any case at all. Ah, and I am plain man enough to think twould be delight to punish them and all of that. But not forever. Not even for long.

"And as regards my friends, are they friends of me indeed? Or of my magic? If I am to be me indeed, and only that, then I am not able to continue being my father's son and being one who is ever to be summoned by my father's horn. Perhaps summoned from peril; true. But perhaps I could by myself defeat that peril.

"Woman!" His voice rang in the silent circle lit by the glimmering moon-maid's lamplight. "Hare!"

She was as cool, serene, as the moon-maid herself. Then as he watched her she grew less so. Her face moved as a true woman's face moves, and changes, and her head sank upon her breast and then she lifted her head again and he saw her tears. "Woman!" she said, in a voice which trembled. "It is long since I have been woman . . ."

He took her arms in his hands and said, his voice low but rough and strong. "You will be woman now. And I will be man."

And he saw her as a woman only, and never as a

queen, and he saw her as a woman only, and never as a hare. She changed, but she did not change to that. Her body was all silver, naked in the moonlight, but her voice in his ear was all gold. Without, she glimmered like silver; within, she flowed like molten gold. She moved beneath him and he moved upon her and they filled and they encompassed one another. In a way it was like entering the bear-death and in all other ways it was nothing like that and nothing like anything else. The sun rose with her and within him and wheeled about in fiery light and the voice he heard in his ears was mightier than any voice of All-Caller. And he was himself and all for himself, as he was all for her, as she was all for him: as no one and as nothing had ever been before.

Later, as he kissed her ears and eyes, her lips and breasts and belly, he thought of the old belief that the lovemaking of the bear does last nine days. And he knew this now to be not so. But was withal well content.

Chapter XVIII

They slept the waning night away wrapped in each other's arms. Dawn found them so, that bride of the locust which does eat up all our days. But no man thinks of that when he is young and in delight of the delights of youth, and it is well that this is so. She did not look old to him in the sunlight, anymore than she had by the shining silver shield of the night. Green was their bed and surrounded by an almost full oval line of trees where a meandering riverlet had transcribed a not-quite-island, along which the deep taproots drank their fill at whatsoever season of the year. Once, at least, the course of the stream had shifted, and left as token of that ancient change a place where there was sand.

"Look you, Arnten," she said, as he sat up and then got to his feet and walked over to join her; "look you," she said, beginning to draw in the sand with a sharp broken stick. "Here is where we are, in this little oval. And"—she raised her ivory hand and the wand in it and moved it a distance and dipped it and drew another line, and this one with an indentation—"this is the safe harbor of which I spoke, by the all-circling sea. And this stream here"—she gestured—"leads into another, and this ..." she paused in her speech but her hand flew swiftly, deftly, surely.

Mered-delfin endeavored almost desperately to show the king, by means of signs which he scratched and lines which he drew. But the king, weak, the king, weary, the king so wan of hope and spent—it seemed—of wit, the king could not follow. The chief witcherer, his face drawn taut as a drumhead by pain and wasting illness, Mered-delfin made squawking noises in his throat and chest, he made buzzing sounds with his thin, parched lips.

The Orfas looked at him with dull, glazed eyes. *"Iron dies,"* he muttered. *"Iron is the matter of the king, and as iron dies, so dies the king ..."*

The chief witcherer buzzed and squawked,

caught the border of the king's robes when his master made as though to lie down again, his eyes leaving the box of sand in which the other made his signs and drew his lines. At length, the Orfas, his face hot and sore with the red scruf which disfigured it and his hands and all his skin as well, the Orfas groaned and half-rose and called in a voice louder than his wont, but a ghost of his former voice. And from behind the reed curtain a voice answered.

"Call the queen," the Orfas said, falling back upon his down pouches and his fleecy coverlets. "Call the queen ... Aye, Mered, Mered, you weary me, and to what end, when there is but one end certain and that is that I must die? Well, call the queen, and let her interpret, if she can. And if not, let her comfort me ... as much as any can. Aye. So," his voice sank low, his eyes turned up. "Call the queen ... call the queen ... call the queen ..."

The sun beat down upon the black spot which was last night's campfire, but Bab slept on as though it were still night. The sun passed over Roke's white skin but though it tarried it seemed not to burn that pale integument. The sun moved its beams along Corm's sallow face and closed eyes, but the eyes did not open. Only Wendolin seemed to sense the sun. Wendolin muttered, lightly, as though asking some riddle in his sleep. Then his face twitched, and he sat bolt upright and gazed around in astonishment. He stooped after a moment and assayed the angle of the sun. "So," he said. "Then he has disengaged himself from us. Well, is it not all the same to me? Let me then get me gone." And he had half risen to his feet and his hands were still flat upon the ground and he frowned as he saw the others. Then he was up, and sighing, and smoothing his garments.

"All the same," he said. "One way or one other way. Then, so, not the way which would mean leaving these here alone." He sighed, he went and set his hand into the old Bab's bundle and withdrew a handful of twigs dried with the leaves still on them and the flowers still in place. He found no flame in the fire and so he made fire a-fresh and then he set this withered bouquet against a coal and whirled it round his head and then he walked thrice round the circle in the whirling smoke, chanting his chant. Then he dropped the smoldering herbs and spat three times upon them. And then he picked them up and cast them into the fire and next he drew open his breeks and made his water upon the fire. And ere it had ceased to sizzle and to steam, the three others had sat them up and were looking round about in puzzlement indeed.

Then, "Where is Bear?" one asked.

"That indeed I know not," said Wendolin, a trifle sadly. "But I know that no common sleep it was which held us all fast-bound here until almost noon, the time of no shadow. Had it reached till then— Well, I know not. But such a deep sleep . . . Who indeed knows the witchery of sleep better than the Bear? Eh?"

The eyes of the others met his own, met each other's, fell. At length, said Roke, "Bear or no, huge or no, still he be but boy."

And his old uncle nodded, and said, more than a trifle sadly, "It may be that his strength came upon

219

him too swift, too soon. A happy childhood and a happy young manhood, he never had: but as a mere cub he was cast into a whirlpool, and he has yet to reach safe shore."

And Corm said nothing, but his mouth settled and his hands reached for All-Caller and he placed the great fey horn to his lips and his cheeks swelled and his lips trembled—

But no sound came out. Helplessly, he offered it to Roke, a flush upon his cheek. But Roke shrank away from it. And then Bab and Wendolin examined it, and then one said, "Ah," and one said, "Oh," and from inside the huge horn which an huger aurochs had once born aloft through every forest in Farthest Thule they extracted a small wad or mass of fur or soft hair or—

"Then what is it?" asked Corm.

Roke gave it a fearful look, then his face cleared and he half-laughed. "Why, tis no witchery but just a jape of sorts," he said, flinging aside his yellow hair to crane for a closer look. "I know it be but the scut of a hare: know ye not that, all?"

Wendolin and Bab nodded, but did not laugh. Corm chuckled, at first in relief, but his relief but echoed Roke's; then puzzlement returned. "What means this, then?" he asked. "And where is your sister's grandchild, old shaman? Did he bewitch us, true? And why? And what is it that we must do?"

There was a silence, and Roke laughed no more, but a color came and went in his skin and for a moment it left the Sign of the Bear outlined upon his scarred breast. "Do? Why—we must follow after and face him, then, and ask what it is he means, and what it is he do not mean: for if he mean to leave we lone and lorn in this Land of Thule, then we be but dead men, all, so long as we do tarry in this Land of Thule."

No one said him nay. And then he spoke again, saying, "And I understand it not, but that I have already died once here, and before I die again, why, I will get me—somehow!—away from this fell Land of Thule.

"If so be that I must swim across the all-circling sea myself."

And later they came to an oval-shaped greensward with a bald of sand in about the center of the lower part of it and this had been much scratched with a stick, it seemed. And at the sight of this both Bab and Wendolin uttered short cries, stilled at once, and they squatted by this bit of sand, and muttered and made witcheries and waved the scut of the hare to the six directions: then Wendolin crouched over and blew and blew, gently, so, so, so, he gently blew, and grain by grain the sand moved: and behind his moving head moved the moving hand of old Bab, grey-white with the white-grey ash the hand bore, scattering ash, letting it sift slowly down, slow, so slow, so, so . . .

"A map!" Corm exclaimed, in wonder.

"By this trail moved the Bear," old Bab began—when a sound which was not a sound was not so much heard as felt, in their inner ears and on the outer air.

Said Roke, uneasy: "What was that?"

And Wendolin: "That was the intended breaking of the spell which I broke earlier, else we had all still been there where we were last night. So, then, that at least is well, that he did not intend us to remain bewitched there forever and until the snows froze us or the spotted ounces dug us from the snow for their food."

Said Roke, slowly, his fingers fretting upon his scars and the weals of his wounds, "That is well, then, yes. But it will be weller when we can look him face to face and ask: Be you man or bear or boy: and what do you mean for us, whichever?"

"You are my woman, then," said Arnten, taking her by the arms and turning her about to face him. Her face had been calm and now it seemed suffused with joy; it had been pale and now it took on the faint, faint color of the wild rose.

"I am yours," she said.

"And I may take and have you when I want," he said, speaking with a roughness which he was far from feeling.

"I am yours in all things and at all times," she said.

He said, still rough, but his voice now and then loosening into a tremor, "Then I will have you now, and here and now, and they had better not come spying on me or calling me, or—"

But her mouth was on his and he forgot what he had intended to threaten.

Afterwards, he said, intending to sound scornful but instead sounding only happy, "Well, and am I better than that rusty old wolf?" She hid her face against him and gently took his skin between her teeth. Then she released him and she nodded. Swiftly looked up, a sheen upon her own skin, swiftly nodded again, shyly smiled; again hid her face. "And," he asked, boldly, defiantly, and again would-be-scornfully and happily, "And does he shoot rusty loads as well?"

She leaned her head up towards his, her neck stretching, and he bent down to kiss one pulse which trembled in the hollow of her throat and she jumped and gasped and then he bent his head still lower and he heard her whisper in his ear and he raised his head and his throat swelled with his howl of triumphant laughter.

"What? None at all?" he bellowed. And her face lit up with a glee which he had never before seen and perhaps few others had ever seen either, and she nodded: and he laughed again. And again. And he crushed her in his arms, and he laughed, and he laughed, and he laughed.

Chapter XIX

Mered-delfin heard her laughing as he moved slowly down from the north. He made signs, and the captains of the kingsmen nodded.

Wendolin and Corm and Roke and Bab heard it, approaching with stealth from the west.

She laughed there upon the deck of the largest of her three vessels in the hidden cove. She had sent the sailingmen away a distance, to the south. They were strange to Arnten's eyes, those twenty men, squat and strong, with shiny black hair and grey eyes and tiny rings in their ears: they had bowed down at the sight of her. And then they had talked, swift-worded, together, and then they had all bowed down to him. And then she had sent them a distance away, to the south.

"They will return before dawn tomorrow," she said.

"So."

"I should have wished to go now, even now, even before now. But they said twas best to take the dawn-tide."

He said, "So," and spread fleeces on the deck and snuffed up the scent of land and of river and of sea.

"There are good winds at this season, and we shall cross the all-circling sea sooner than you might believe. And then whither, eh?" she asked.

He began to pluck at her garments, he had not yet gained deftness at this, but perhaps she preferred it so. Certainly she preferred to pretend that she knew not what he was about. And as he fumbled, she asked, "Shall we intend for the nearest port and sell our furs and amber and ivory and gold at heavy prices, it having been long since any treasure cargoes have reached there from hence?"

"My treasure-cargo is here," he muttered. And tugged. And, she not moving, he lifted her up with a sigh of impatience, and tugged and slipped the clinging cloth away, and then he touched her in wonder, and, wondering, watched her touch him.

And she had laughed, exulting.

They heard her laugh, the sailingmen, a distance away to the south, and they grinned at each other and they ate their roasts of the wild sheep which they had hunted: and next they cast the shoulder blades of the sheep upon the fire: and watched the omen-telling cracks appear: and then they pulled long faces and they shook their heads. And they examined their weapons by the firelight and in the gathering dusk, exclaimed at the tell-tale signs of the iron pox which afflicted this odd, strange land of Thule: and they muttered their relief that they would leave it soon; to be exact, at next dawn-tide. And then they glanced again at the cracked shoulder blades and again they shook their heads.

So it was that, as the two lovers lay upon their bed upon the deck of the ship, their fingers and the locks of their hair twining together and watching the pale stars come to peer through the veil of night and minding not the first faint fall of dew, that a one or two things made them pause. He felt her grow tense. He sat upright, growling.

She said, "What—"

He said, "Did you hear it, too? It is that one called Corm, he knew me as I was a boy, and remains but still a boy himself, and thinks—they all think—that I am yet to be controlled as one controls a boy . . ."

She said, "What—"

He said, "It is that horn of my father's which I let Corm bear for me and so he may think tis his, which tis not, the horn called *fey*, called *All-caller*—"

She said, "Ahhh . . ."

"And now he dares not blow it full, but his lips breathe a riff of air into its mouth, and that is what I hear, and it fills me full with rage: that still they follow after me and will not let me be free. They come. They are near."

And she said, "Did I not speak to my own

sailingmen, bidding them be gone till dawn-light? Yet they approach: Hear."

There was the sound of a strange call of a bird which had never nested in the Land of Thule. "Tis their signal," she said. "How do they dare? Is disobedience abroad on every breeze tonight? They come. They are near."

Without other word the two of them dressed themselves and arose and peered into the dimness and the dark. And it seemed that the dim and the darkness peered back at them, and that something moved therein.

Arnten said, grim, and growling in his chest, "I know who you be, your faces I need not see, for I know your tread and I snuff your smell. What, Roke! What, Corm! What, my mother's uncle! And what—you youngling nain whose name my tongue would trip upon! And what—you wizard Wendolin! Listen, all. I am not that bear who may be ringed through the septum of his nose and trained to dance upon the tug of a rope, do thee hear, every which one of thee?"

"Thy weird, Bear," a voice from the night began, slowly.

"My weird!" he cried. "I cry scorn upon my weird as you be-think it! My weird now and for some time since and for all time hence, my weird be what *I* shall make it. You have pressed and followed me too close with your mumble and your snuffle of *My weird, Thy weird, His weird,* and *That one's weird.*"

"Thy father," another voice began: and he growled more fiercely, even, against this other voice.

226

"My father, aye! My father, true! My father, so! Woe was upon my father that he suffered his weird to fall into the hands of wizards, nains, witcherers, and indeed of any in the Land of Thule. He ought never to have returned unto the Land of Thule, and this I shall tell thee all: Does my weird suffer me to escape this Land of Thule, curse me from the day that ever I return to it, as was my father cursed ever from that day that *he* returned to it?"

And, soft from the darkness: "Thy father's curse, O Bear, do stand upon the ship beside thee . . ."

"Oh, lie!" she cried—and then the strange bird-call sounded clear, and sounded near, and with relief she cupped her hands and called, "Hither, hither, faster, and hither to me!" And the other figures melted back into the bosky and the black as, by one and by two and three, the squat, stout sailingmen appeared.

"O Mistress," one began.

"I forgive your disobedience," she said, "in returning so long before the time I said: only get you now unto your several ships and hoist the anchor-stones: if there is as yet no wind, no tide, then pole us out at least a way to sea, for—"

And the captain-chief of the small fleet, coming nearer and bowing low, said, "This, Mistress, is what we would hear you say, for on casting the shoulder blades of the wild sheep into our evening fire, we saw malign configurations appear as the lines of fortune and of weird appeared when the heat o' the fire produced the cracks of predication. Exceeding strange they were, and—"

A sound broke in upon his words, rose upon the

shuddering air, ululated, fell away; and twice more was repeated.

"A wolf—"

"The wolf!"

From afar, but yet not far, other men's voices—

"*The wolf! The wolf! The Orfas! King Orfas!*" and, "*His men! Kingsmen! King Orfas!*", and, "*The wolf!*" cried Arnten's men.

She said, "To sea— At once, at once—to sea—"

"No, now, not so swift and soon," Arnten said. "To sea, and soon, yes. But not so soon that I do not sooner settle what lies between me and this wolf-king, for as my father—"

And she, hot-swift, her hand clasped on his, and stronger her grip than ever he would have thought, whilst still the howling wolf came nearer and the enemy voices clamored from the wood; she: "Ah, Bear! By my body and by yours! This accursed stubbornness of thy seed and blood! Did I not years gone by beg your father to get us gone together away from wolf and Thule? And he would tarry and he would fight, and see what that but brought him! And long I'd thought him gone from Thule across the all-circling sea without me and I waited, waited, dured long and woefully without him, till the old chief smith of all the nains persuaded me that twas not so that all the nains were in cabal with him to curse iron that he might then return— And so— And then—" her words tumbled in confusion and he tugged, impatient.

She mastered her mouth, and said, clear, "So then I knew he must still be here in Thule, and if none of all our spying had espied him as a man, then— So I had the kingsmen sent out, for I asked of the hares and I asked of the salmon and the bees, and they told me where, the Bear—"

Now he broke her grip as twas grass, and now he gripped her and he said, low, "So twas thee encompassed his captivity, and mine?"

"Only that I might confront him and again offer him—"

"Then twas because of *thee* he died!"

"I never wished him dead, only that he and I might go forever gone, as now I want that thee and I—"

Arn's voice was grom, and his hand tightened upon hers and he said, "Because of *thee* he died: So."

And then she cried out, astonishment greater than pain or fear, and pointed, pointed with her other free hand. And every voice was stilled, afar as well as near. Then every voice broke loud again, in shock, in fear, in wonder great.

Across the sky from past the dripping stars a fiery spear was hurled, and then after it another, and another, and from every quarter of the sky came fiery spear, arching across the sky and falling, falling, falling, hurling down to earth.

The sailingmen uttered together one sound like the wail of a babe torn brutely from a mother's breast and they fell face down where they had stood, and buried their faces in their arms. But Arn shouted a great high shout of understanding and of triumph, and Corm raised All-Caller to his lips, and Wendolin laughed aloud in wizard-glee and Bab danced and croaked and pointed, and even the silent nain lifted his heavy head and bayed at the sky; and Roke beat his hands upon his breast and stamped with his feet upon the ground. And all the sky was filled with the light of the falling fire-streaks and sound of rumbling and above all of this rose Arn's voice.

" 'When the stars throw down their spears and pelt the earth with thunderstones'—See now? See now! See how the stars throw down their spears— hear how they pelt the earth with thunderstones—"

One after the other the burning spears hurtled, crashing, into the ground, and Arn marked the quarter of their crashing, noted the section of their fall; and still the angry stars hurled more. Arn took one stride to where the pot of coals rested on sand and on stones and slowly turned to ashes, there safe in its nest at the bow of the ship. And he stepped over her as though she were not there as she lay there, moaning in terror, and he ripped up handfuls of tow and tinder as he strode, and he blew upon the grey embers and saw them flash into light and life. And he snatched at the quiver and the bow. And he called to the captain-chief of the sailingmen.

Little indeed in those moments did that one think that ever he would see again his home across the all-circling sea and had no other thought but that he would die, and directly, there in the fell Land of Thule, crushed and burned to death by the fall of heaven—as so he and they, his mates, did think it. But out of the fear and doom and terror of that while a horn sounded and a voice called him by title and there was in that voice somewhat which bade him not tarry. He rose to his feet, he hearkened, half-understanding, he kicked his mates, and they all rose up and went stumbling to the ships.

There was the lover of their mistress, and he seemed grown exceeding great and he spoke in a voice like the voice of thunder and they noticed now of great sudden that the pelt he wore was the pelt of the bear and it be-thought them how he was very Bear indeed and perhaps that same Bear whose stars trod the skies of heaven: he gave them orders, they swarmed up and they obeyed.

"Fire against fire!" he cried. "Shoot up that way! And over there! And over there! Good! Good! As long as arrows and tow and tinder and earth-fire hold out, continue your shooting; and you will indeed see victory—"

They, half-numbly at first, and then with growing zeal, wrapped tow and tinder round their arrows' heads and dipped them in the pot of coals and fired them off whither he, this Bear, had directed. And from the fire-flecked darkness a ways off came cries of terror and alarm, of horror, fright, and flight. For the star-spears fell not that close at all (but Arn and his company marked where they were falling), fell farther off by far from where the kingsmen lay huddled in terror. But when the sailingmen shot off their own burning arrows at the sky, why ... what goeth up must in time come down ... And come down the shipmen's arrows did. And all about the place where the wolf had howled and where the men of the wolf had huddled. It was all the same to them: they did not pause to consider if one or if two different kind of fiery missile came down at them from the burning sky. They fled. They left spear and club and every

231

weapon indeed, and they fled. And they howled as they fled. But it was not the menacing howl of the great wolf.

And in a while the time came, as Arn had known it would, that the stars began to slacken in their hurling of fire-spears and of thunderstones. And when the ships men saw this, they shouted in fierce triumph, and had no further doubts but that—and thanks to the wisdom of the Bear—they had indeed fought fire with fire. So they shouted and seized fresh arrows and wound tinder and tow about their heads and dipped them in the pot of glowing coals and nocked them into their bows and shot them, cursing and gleeing, towards the fleeing stars; shouting to each other and to their mistress and her leman, this great Bear, that they had put and were still putting the stars to flight: and would soon have them driven back to their own country once and for all.

Arn had not noticed her as she crept across the deck, had not felt her grasp his leg; only now when he turned—without word—to go, did he feel her. And he muttered and would have shaken her loose.

"O Bear! By my body and by yours! Whither do you go? And why?" she begged.

He was of no mind to return reply to this witless question, but it seemed simpler to speak than to grapple. "I was wrong, see you, about my weird," he said. "It lies here in this Land of Thule, it was but slow in coming, slow to show itself," he said. "My weird is iron. See now how the time for the curing of the sickness unto death of iron has arrived? The stars, don't thee see?" he burst out at her. "The stars have cast down spears at earth, and spears be made of iron, yea or nay? Be sure that the stars have no sickness among them. Be sure that we shall be-cure our iron by means of the fresh, hot, and healthy iron of the star-spears. Be sure—"

She moaned and shook her head. She clung to him. Again he recollected that twas she to whom he owed his father's death, but he was not minded yet to savage or to slay her. Was she ravaged with grief and pain? Off and away with her, then! Let her get herself and her hare's scut gone—

"Arnten, Arnten, Arn!" she cried, clinging to him. "Thy weird be iron, but iron is also the weird of the king! As iron was dying, so was the king dying. And if it be that thee cure iron while he does live, Arnten, Arnten, Arn, do ye not see, all of ye, thee and thy fellows— *If you cure iron, then you cure the king!*"

He stood there, stock-still, his mouth agape, and looked at her. The truth of her words transfixed him. To do and to undo! To repeat it all again, then? Once more to be the enemy and flee the wrath of that kinsman who hated him more than any stranger? Fights and flights and long and weary journeyings . . .

The captain-chief, nothing heeding (as nothing knowing) of all these words and all these thoughts, half-turned and flung up his head toward the sky, whence fewer and fewer fire-stones came, and they seeming to drift languidly.

"Eh, master!" cried the captain-chief. "See how they flee! How folk will give thee ward and worship, then, across the sea, when we sail in with word of this great night!"

233

And he gave Arn a half-bow, and he turned and shouted and dipped his arrow in the fire and let fly his shaft.

What, then, was weird, what was indeed his fate, what role had he to play? By this latest omen it was to sail with her and her men across the all-circling sea, to find more than mere refuge: to find *rule*! He called into the darkness by the shore, "Bab and Roke and Corm, Wendolin, and thee nain. . . ?"

Let them come aboard. He would not for anything abandon a one of them here. Let them come with him across the sea and begin life new: and a curse to Thule and all its thrall-weirds.

"Bear and Son of the Bear," said one voice.

"Star-sender," said one voice.

"Star-disperser," said another.

"Star-finder," said a next one.

"Finder of Star-spears, Heater of Forges, Forger of Fire-born, Seer of the Sorrows of the Land and Freer of this Land from Sorrows . . ."

He said, "Aboard of this vessel." He watched as they came. The woman's face glowed. Then her eyes met his in the brief flare of the tinder and the swift glare of the tow. And he saw that she knew, and he saw that her hopes were dead and he saw that her age was full upon her. The dawn now sailed up from the sea and its pale lamp replaced the flash-flash-flash of star-spear and fire-arrows. He said, "Captain-chief."

"Master. Bear."

He said: "Past this harbor is a headland and past that is another and past that is a river-mouth. Thither we will go."

The chief sailingman nodded.

"There you may leave us, and return to your own country, or you or any of you who wish may remain with us and fare if they will with us."

The sailingman scanned the tide and the shore and turned a bit and gazed off as if laying out a voyage in his mind's eye. "In that direction, then, Bear, you will go?"—he moved his hand— "To that way whither the stars hurled down their spears?—and where, I must suppose, those fiery spears may still be found?"

Arn said, "Yes. It is there."

Author's note to
URSUS OF ULTIMA THULE

The magic status of the smith and the mingled awe
and horror which attach to it still endures in parts
of Africa, where the ironworker is sometimes—at
least till not so long ago—the priest as well; and
sometimes believed to be a were-hyaena. It may
be, then, that in African folk-lore the hyaena does
for the wolf just as in the folk-lore of southern Europe the wolf occupied the place taken in northern
Europe by the bear. I have not ever seen in any
folk-lore a connection between iron-magic and
bear-magic, but in this book I have ventured to
close that gap in the circle. The motif of The Boy
Who Was Nobody's Son is of course quite common, that of The Boy Who Was The Son of the
Bear is much less common. This commingling of
the two elements is as far as I know unique, at
least in modern writing. I am indebted to Dr.
François Bordes of the Bordeaux Museum of
Pre-History for a personal relation of the French
legend of *Jean-à-l'ourse*; and to Prof. Rhys Car-
penter's book, *Folk Tale, Fiction and Saga in the
Homeric Epics* (U. of Cal. Press, 1958).